PRAISE FOR
NANCY BOYARSKY'S
NICOLE GRAVES MYSTERIES

"full of page-by-page surprises"
–*Kirkus Reviews*

"a charming and straight-shooting heroine…nail-biting
adventure whose thralls are difficult to escape"
–*Foreword Reviews*

"a hold-onto-the-bar roller coaster of a mystery"
–*RT Book Reviews*

"Nicole Graves is the best fictional sleuth to come down the pike
since Sue Grafton's Kinsey Millhone."
–Laura Levine, author of the popular *Jaine Austen Mysteries*

"Well written, non-stop, can't-put-it-down suspense."
–Charles Rosenberg, bestselling author of *Death on a High Floor*

"Well developed characters in a rich English setting brings ample
twists throughout and all the way to the final pages."
–Eric Hoffer Award Gold Medal Winner 2018 for *The Swap*

THE

BIG SHAKEUP

a Nicole Graves mystery

THE

BIG SHAKEUP

a Nicole Graves mystery

NANCY BOYARSKY

 Light Messages

Published 2023, by Light Messages
www.lightmessages.com
Durham, NC 27713 USA
SAN: 920-9298

Paperback ISBN: 978-1-61153-531-0
Ebook ISBN: 978-1-61153-532-7
Library of Congress Control Number: 2023939872

For the people I love most:
Bill, Jennie, John, Anabelle, and Lila.
And in loving memory of Robin

CHAPTER ONE

NICOLE ARRIVED AT COLBERT AND SMITH INVESTIGATIONS as dawn was breaking. She hoped that if she got to the office early, she'd have a few hours to catch up with her work before the firm's investigators, many of them new, arrived and demanded her attention.

As she waited for the elevator, she heard a sound and turned to look. Someone was slipping into the stairwell leading to the garage. All she saw was an arm and a leg as the door closed, not even enough to tell if the stranger was male or female. He, or she, was wearing dark clothes and seemed in an enormous hurry. Odd, she thought. Who would be sneaking out of the building at this hour? It could, she supposed, be one of the homeless whose tents and broken-down vans lined the nearby streets. On the other hand, several of the building's suites had suffered after-hours break-ins. Could this be the perp? Only when she pulled out her phone to call the building's management office did she remember the time. No one would be there this early.

Still perturbed, she got in the elevator and punched the button for the top floor. Once inside the firm's suite, she passed through reception and the empty bullpen where the investigators worked. Entering the hallway leading to her office, she saw that her boss's office lights were on. She wasn't surprised. Jerry had been sleeping there for several weeks. She took it as a sign that his marriage was failing under the weight of his gambling, drinking, and general decline in behavior.

They'd been friends—good friends—for most of the time she'd worked here. In those days, he would have told her if there was trouble between him and Melanie. But their friendship had cooled in recent months. Now things were less than cordial, and their chats and confidences had ended. Instead of going down the hall and announcing her arrival, she went into her own office and quietly closed the door.

She settled at the desk and thought about her job, how deeply unsatisfying it had become since Jerry had promoted her to vice president. He'd raised her salary, but that didn't make up for the tediousness of her duties as a glorified office manager. She was good at managing people, but she'd had the same job years before and had burned out. That was why she became a P.I. in the first place. Investigating cases had been interesting and sometimes exciting. But shuffling paperwork, handing cases over to underlings, and dealing with their problems was another story.

With the bad blood between her and her boss, she'd wanted to resign. But her life had been too chaotic. She was engaged to Ronald Reinhardt, a former MI6 agent. They'd had to reschedule their wedding date several times. Now she was busy setting it up again. Looking for a new job at the same time would be a nightmare.

The week before, she'd been unable to resist a juicy missing-persons case. Instead of handing it over to one of her reports, she'd kept it for herself. It had been worth the extra effort, but it had taken up most of the week. Now her monthly report was due, with just a few days to make up the time she'd lost.

All at once she heard a faint tapping noise. Looking around her desk, she saw that her globe paperweight was vibrating against the base of her desk lamp. Through the doorway to the hall, the dangling light fixture was swaying. Panicked by the thought of an earthquake, she stood up. Hoping to reassure herself, she turned to look out the window. But the scene outside was anything but reassuring. The telephone poles and skinny-trunked palm trees across the street were shaking, and a low rumble had started up.

The scary part of an earthquake is that there's no way to predict how big it will get. As a native Californian, she'd been through enough of them to know what might happen next. Most quakes wound down shortly and ranked five or six points on the Richter Scale—enough to knock things off shelves, break some chimneys, and cause some injuries. On the other hand, it could keep growing until it destroyed everything it touched. It had been over a century since the last truly destructive earthquake had flattened San Francisco. But geologists had been warning that "The Big One" was on its way.

The shaking kept growing more intense. Books flew off the shelves. Nicole dove under the desk. Seconds later, one of her cabinets fell over, crashing into the spot where she'd been sitting. The doors of the other cabinets flew open, dumping their contents on the floor. Ceiling tiles rained down.

Nicole had a flashback to the only major earthquake she'd ever experienced—the Northridge quake of 1994. She'd been a young child at the time, and the experience remained one of her most vivid memories. It had been substantial, a 6.7, and she recalled her sense of terror and helplessness as her room seemed to tilt and sway, and her mother screaming and bursting through the wobbling doorframe to grab her and hold her close.

Back in the present, the shaking was still gathering force. She crawled further into the desk's knee space, tried to brace herself and grip its legs. Holding on was next to impossible when the desk jumped with every jolt. Even more frightening was the noise. It had started as a rumble but now sounded like the roar of an oncoming train.

Every instinct told her to run, get out of the building. But with so much movement, she knew she'd never be able to stand up, much less run down eight flights of stairs. As the shaking continued to build, all thought disappeared. Later she was surprised to learn the whole thing had lasted a mere three-and-a-half minutes. But, if she knew anything at the time, it was that the shaking would go on until the building collapsed and buried her.

Almost as quickly as it had begun, the quake's violent movement eased into a trembling, rocking motion, like a ship in a choppy sea. After a series of weak shudders, it stopped. She found herself on her hands and knees, panting for breath. Once all was still, she climbed out from under the desk.

Her office was a disaster. Shards of window glass were all over the floor along with the ceiling tiles and everything that had been on her desk, inside her cabinets, and on top of them. Wires hung down through gaps in the ceiling. The lights she'd turned on a few minutes before were now off. Her desk chair and the two in front of her desk were on their backs. Nothing was where it was supposed to be.

She thought of Reinhardt, her fiancée. He was in London on an assignment for his employer, the British Consulate in Los Angeles. With today's instant communications, he was sure to learn of the quake within minutes, if not seconds. She had to let him know she was all right. She looked around for her phone. It was on the floor, its cord caught under one end of the desk. She couldn't loosen it, and the desk was too heavy to lift, so she squatted down and picked up the receiver. There was no dial tone—of course, since the lights were off, the power had failed. No doubt the quake had also knocked down cellular towers and telephone switching stations.

Her purse had bounced off her desk and was barely visible under a layer of fallen debris. She picked it up, got out her cell phone, and tried the call again. She heard a busy signal before she finished putting in his number. She thought of Stephanie, her sister. Was she okay? She remembered a news story—one of many since a six-point earthquake in Northern California had given people the jitters—explaining what to do in case of a major quake. She was supposed to send a text message instead of trying to call. She sent messages to Reinhardt and her sister. In theory, the system would keep trying to deliver them until they got through—whenever that might be.

Dropping her cell in her pocket, Nicole stepped over to the window. Most of the glass was gone, and a chilly breeze swept in. Only now did she notice the racket outside, a cacophony of sirens, building alarms, and helicopters. She was stunned to see all the destruction on her block alone. The twelve-story building across the street had pancaked and was now only five or six stories; it was hard to tell. Lower levels were delineated only by lines where floors and ceilings met. If any of the building's employees had come to work as early as she, most would be dead. A trio of long-legged palm trees planted across the street had keeled over and sprawled across the boulevard. Looking down, Nicole could see their mop tops resting against her building.

All at once she thought of Jerry. He hadn't stirred from his office. She couldn't imagine why he hadn't come out to check on his firm's office suite, which was a great source of pride to him. Had he been injured? Something worse?

She'd been angry with him over a recent row that had been witnessed by just about everyone in the office. It had started when Nicole pointed out that Jerry's management failures had been the cause of the firm's ever-increasing cash-flow problems. Once again, they'd had to delay handing out paychecks to the thirty-odd employees, this time for at least two weeks.

The fight between Nicole and Jerry had escalated and become physical. In front of the office staff, Jerry—visibly under the influence—accused Nicole of sabotaging the agency, even stealing from it. When words failed, he tried to punch her. He was so drunk that he missed and staggered against her, almost knocking her over. So unpopular had Jerry become that Nicole's coworkers were rooting for her. She retaliated to his aggression with a solid punch to his nose. The blow had drawn blood, but at that point, Jerry was flat on the floor, beyond caring.

Nicole walked away, resolved to quit that very moment. She hoped she wouldn't have too much trouble finding work. She was well known among the city's corporate investigation firms. She also had notoriety from her involvement in several high-profile cases that had gone viral in the media. In one incident, she'd briefly been "a person of interest" in the death of an office mate who'd left her a fortune at what had turned out to be a very inconvenient moment.

Stories about her had appeared in the press. As a very private person, she'd been upset by this. She hated seeing her name and photo in the paper and on various news outlets. But those headlines, along with her professional reputation, had resulted in some rather good job offers at the time. Now she felt like kicking herself for not accepting one.

She'd written her resignation letter and was clearing out her desk when Jerry, a bit wobbly on his feet, came in to apologize. Trying to convince her to stay, he offered her a substantial raise the firm could ill afford—more proof that he was still drunk.

When she refused, he looked as if he were about to cry. "Please, Nicole. I'm so sorry. I don't know what got into me. No one else can do what you can. Won't you stay long enough to find a replacement and train them? I'm begging you." He got down on one knee and looked at her beseechingly.

Nicole was annoyed by his theatrics. "For God's sake, get up," she said. "I'll stay long enough to find a replacement and write a manual explaining my job. But that's it."

Jerry awkwardly got back to his feet, gave her a pat on the shoulder, and shuffled out of her office. Nicole immediately placed hiring notices on local bulletin boards, as well as on LinkedIn. In a few days, she began interviewing applicants.

But now—worried about his safety—her anger was, for the most part, gone. She walked cautiously down the hall, thinking that all that shaking might have destabilized the building. But the floor felt solid enough. She arrived at Jerry's door and surveyed the ruin of his office, which was in worse shape than hers. His desk was on its side. Papers, file folders, office supplies, ceiling tiles, and shards of broken windows were strewn everywhere. Jerry himself seemed to be missing.

Nicole looked around. She went to his bathroom and knocked. The door, unlocked, swung open. He wasn't there. Only then did she think to look behind the desk.

He was lying on the floor. When she called his name, he didn't respond. As she walked toward him, she saw the pool of blood around his head. Bending down for a closer look, she noticed a black object half hidden beneath him. She bent down to pull it out and was stunned to see it was a gun. Did that mean the earthquake hadn't killed him? That he'd been shot?

She hadn't heard a gun go off, which meant it must have happened before the quake and before she arrived. As she tossed the gun aside, she realized she'd seen it before. It was when he'd asked her to look through his desk to see if he'd left his phone there. He hadn't, but she happened on the gun in the top left-hand drawer of his desk. She'd checked, and it was loaded. At the time, she'd wondered who or what he was afraid of. Now she realized he must have shot himself.

With great effort, she turned him onto his back. The sight of his injuries made her feel sick. His head was a bloody mess. One of his ears was missing along with a chunk of jaw.

She bent down to put her head to his chest, listening for a heartbeat. She could barely make one out, along with a bubbling, wheezing sound she supposed was an effort to breathe. She wondered if pressure on the wound might stop the bleeding. Then she remembered what she'd learned in an office first-aid class. Never apply pressure to a head wound that might have penetrated the skull. With all that blood, how could she tell? She had to find a doctor or paramedic before Jerry bled out.

A door slammed. She heard footsteps and the low voices of a man and woman as they made their way through the bullpen. They seemed to be arguing. Their words were indecipherable until the woman yelled, "I'm not going back in there. Let go of me!"

"It's for your own peace of mind," the man said. "Just take a quick look. What you heard was probably a car backfiring."

Now that they were closer, Nicole recognized their voices. Diana Chang was her most recent hire, a recent college grad who'd accepted a job as a secretary in hope of eventually qualifying as a private investigator. The man, Nate Goodwin, one of the firm's long-time investigators. He was a relentless womanizer, always hitting on the youngest of the new hires. He was forty to Diana's twenty-three. Still, no one had ever complained about his behavior.

"It's Nicole!" she called out. "I'm in Jerry's office!"

Diana, a pretty, fine-boned creature, appeared in the doorway. "Is everything alright?" she said.

Nicole silently gestured toward Jerry's still form.

When Diana caught sight of him, she screamed, "Oh God! Oh, no!" Bursting into tears, she disappeared back into the hallway. Meanwhile Nate walked in, stood over the body, and studied it.

Seconds later, they heard the sound of Diana vomiting. Nicole remembered how upbeat the young woman usually was. She seemed to like Jerry even when everyone else had turned on him. She'd laughed at his lame jokes and seemed fascinated by everything he said. Nicole could understand why she'd be upset by the sight of his body.

Nate ignored Diana's outburst and kept staring at Jerry. "Is he dead? Was it the quake? Like, something fell on him?"

"I think he's still breathing," Nicole said. "He was shot with his own gun. I think he tried to kill himself. I need to get him medical attention. Can you stay with him while I run downstairs and flag down an emergency van?"

Nate looked up in surprise. "*Stay* with him? Um—I don't think—I mean, what if he died while I was here alone with him? I'm sorry, but—"

"Alright. What about Diana? Where is she?"

"No idea, but she'd be useless here. One look at Jerry, and she barfed."

Nicole and Nate left the office together. Diana was nowhere to be found. Taking an elevator was out of the question. Even without the threat of an aftershock, elevators couldn't operate without electricity.

As they cautiously started down the stairs, Nicole said, "Why did you and Diana come to the office so early?"

"We were at an after-hours club last night," he said. "I guess we had too much to drink. Diana said she wasn't feeling well, and she left first. Said she wasn't up to driving so she was coming here for the rest of the night. I don't even remember going back to my place, but that's where I woke up. I came in to check on her. When I got here, she was freaking out about something."

They'd reached the second-floor landing. Nicole was about to ask Nate what Diana had told him. Had she seen something or heard the shot that killed Jerry?

Just then, the shaking started up again. It felt as if the walls were closing in. Only then did Nicole notice deep cracks in the walls and ceiling. Just as suddenly as it began, the shaking stopped. She turned and there was Nate, half a flight behind. He was sitting on a step, shielding his head with his arms.

She started down again. When she reached the street, squad cars, fire engines, and paramedic vans were speeding by, sirens screaming.

Nicole began to wave at passing vehicles just as Nate bolted from the building. To her surprise, he kept running and, without a word, disappeared around the corner.

Okay, she thought. He hadn't been much help. Now that he was gone, she had one less person to worry about. Her thoughts shifted to Jerry's wife. Melanie had been coming in to do the firm's books for the last several months. She and Nicole had gone out to lunch a few times. Melanie had a way of deflecting unpleasant topics. She never complained about Jerry. When his name came up, she changed the subject.

As far as Nicole could see, the couple's relationship was broken. They didn't speak or interact when they were in the office at the same time— no surprise with Jerry's recent behavior—booze and drugs, a major gambling addiction, and failure to manage the firm, which was his and Melanie's main asset. There were also the women who called the firm looking for him, not on business but on what they called "something personal."

Nicole thought of Melanie and their twin boys, still toddlers. If Jerry died—and she didn't see how he could survive—what would become of them?

Each time an emergency vehicle approached, she stepped off the curb and waved her arms. But none of them even slowed. The situation seemed hopeless. She made a last try, half-heartedly waving at an approaching paramedic van. She was surprised when it pulled over, and the driver rolled down the passenger window.

Nicole turned to gesture at her office building. "A man is severely injured up there," she said. "Eighth floor."

The driver was alone in the van. "Was it the quake?" he said.

"No. It's a gunshot wound."

"Hundreds are buried under buildings. Rescuing the living is our top priority. Are you sure he's still alive?"

"He was a few minutes ago."

The driver stepped out of the van, a tall Latino in a tight T-shirt that emphasized his bulging muscles. He grabbed a folding gurney from the back of the van along with a medical bag. "Is that building stable?"

Nicole thought of the cracks in the stairwell. "I didn't have any problem coming down the stairs."

He disappeared inside, pulling the gurney behind him.

Nicole waited. No longer focused on flagging down help, she took in the devastation around her. Her own building, the eight-story Wilshire Tower left over from the art deco revival in the 1920s, was still standing. Many other buildings were not. It was hard to believe this newly formed hellscape was real.

A few single-story structures had caved in or hopped off their foundations. The newer skyscrapers had fared much worse. Some had toppled, partially crumbling into piles of rubble. Others had pancaked, leaving a thin line to mark where an entire floor had folded in on itself and disappeared. The smell of smoke and leaking gas made it hard to breathe. This brought to mind something she'd read, that fire and gas explosions were the biggest threat after a quake. As if on cue, she heard a loud blast and turned to see a dark cloud rise a few blocks away.

Once again, she felt the urge to run. This was tempered by her need to know Jerry's fate. Would the paramedic come out pushing him on the gurney or was he dead?

It wasn't long before he was back with the still-empty gurney. "Sorry, but your friend didn't make it. Give me your contact information and his, if you have it. I'll let the authorities know. By the way, the building doesn't seem stable. I wouldn't go back inside if I were you."

Nicole gave him Jerry's information, as well as her own. The van drove off, and she started home, grateful that the townhouse she shared with Reinhardt was within walking distance. Turning the first corner, she stopped and stared at the huge, deep gash the quake had torn down the center of the street. The sidewalk was still passable, and she kept going. There were more fallen telephone poles, tangles of cables and downed power lines that lay across sidewalks and streets. Part of her held a sliver of hope that this was a bad dream, that she'd wake up and everything would be back to normal.

When she reached home, she went from room to room, surveying the damage. Their possessions were scattered everywhere, the carpets covered with broken glass and china, shattered vases and paintings that had fallen off the walls. Table lamps and light-weight furniture had toppled over. In the kitchen, every bottle, jar and box had crashed to the floor. Most had broken open and spilled their contents. The refrigerator had fallen forward and was at a diagonal, with its doors resting against the opposite counter.

Nicole went upstairs to change into jeans and a T-shirt. This taken care of, she tried again to reach Melanie to tell her about Jerry's death, then felt guilty at her relief when she got a busy signal.

She checked her text messages, but neither Reinhardt nor her sister had responded to hers. Although she knew it was pointless, she tried turning on the lights, then the TV. But the electricity was out here, just as it had been at the office. A wave of exhaustion swept over her, and she decided that—at least for a few minutes—she'd better get off her feet and try to recharge. She went upstairs, cleared a path through the fallen debris, and swept away chunks of the ceiling that had fallen on the bed. After kicking off her shoes, she lay down. Moments later, the place started shaking. She jumped out of bed, ready to dive underneath. By then, the aftershock had stopped.

Too rattled to lie down or even sit, she went out on the balcony to look at the city. In at least half a dozen spots, smoke was rising. A huge cloud of smoke hovered over downtown L.A. She wondered what was burning. One of the big fifty-floor office buildings, or a hotel? God help anyone trapped on an upper floor.

When the place started shaking yet again, she stepped back inside and braced herself against the wall. But it was just another brief aftershock. Even though she knew to expect them, they always inspired the same feeling of terror. She thought how lovely it would be if she were in London with Reinhardt. His trip had been a last-minute assignment that left him with barely enough time to pack. He'd wanted her to come with him. She'd fallen behind at work and needed a few days to catch up. But she promised to join him on the weekend. If only she'd had the foresight to leave when he did, she'd have escaped this nightmare. She could have kept an eye on the situation and returned when the city became livable again.

She found herself going over her conversation with him about his trip for the consulate. When she asked what his assignment was, he'd demurred. "It involves a trade agreement, pretty routine stuff," he'd said. "I'll spare you the details. But it won't take more than a week. If you can join me, we can visit Spain or the south of France when I'm done."

This sounded wonderful, but she couldn't help worrying about the nature of his assignment. The vagueness of his reply was similar to the way he used to explain his long absences when he was a covert operative for MI6. His unpredictable disappearances had been a major source of conflict between them. He couldn't seem to understand why she objected.

Finally, Nicole had told him she couldn't live that way anymore, never knowing when he was going to disappear and, once gone, if he was ever coming back. Besides that, she wanted marriage, children, a normal family life, while he was unable to give up the excitement and danger of being a covert operative. She told him she'd never marry a spy and was no longer willing to waste the last of her child-bearing years with someone who was never going to settle down.

They didn't communicate for several months. Nicole was heartbroken. Then, to her great surprise, he'd changed his mind. He told her that, after a lot of thought, he realized that he no longer enjoyed his work. He, too, wanted to settle down and start a family. It had been over a year since he'd left the agency. He'd taken the job with the British consulate and moved to L.A. to be with her. She was happy with their life but never quite certain that he was. She worried that he missed being a spy and still yearned for "the life."

He laughed when she brought it up. "You can't imagine how happy I am to be here with you," he'd said. "I'll never go back."

Yet she couldn't accept the idea that Reinhardt was really happy far from home and working in a routine job. She often woke to find him gone, the townhouse empty. When he returned to get ready for work, he explained that he couldn't sleep and enjoyed an early "ramble" to watch the sun come up. She wondered if it was something else. Did he feel trapped? Were these early morning walks the behavior of a caged animal? Was he hiding his discontent, ready to bolt if and when MI6 reached out to him?

And here it was again, her fear that he was ready to leave the moment his former employer reached out. She shook her head to dislodge the thought. She was being ridiculous. He'd invited her to come with him. He wouldn't have done that if he was hoping to be called back to MI6.

She tried to refocus on what might be happening elsewhere in Los Angeles. How hard had other areas been hit? How many had been killed? Injured? What was the magnitude of the earthquake? Surely not a 10. That would have leveled everything. But it might have been an 8. Without electricity, it was impossible to get information from the TV or radio. She tried using her cell, but little words at the top of the screen said, "no service." This total blackout of the news—usually available twenty-four hours a day—was, at least for her, one of the most excruciating aspects of the quake's aftermath.

She doubted the electricity would be back any time soon and regretted not buying a hand-cranked radio for situations like this. Then she remembered her car radio. She went down to the garage and drove the car onto the street, making a wide berth around a gaping crack the quake had torn in the asphalt. She parked, turned on the radio, and sped through the stations. To her great disappointment, all programming had been replaced by static. She was about to return the car to the underground garage. But as she started the engine, she couldn't help thinking of the next possible disaster. What if a strong aftershock made the townhouse collapse? Her car would be buried underneath. She left it parked on the street.

She got out her emergency supplies—flashlights, batteries, candles, matches—from the cupboards and left them on the kitchen table so they'd be easy to find when it grew dark. Her next chore was to clear out the refrigerator before the food spoiled. Only when she went into the kitchen did she remember the fridge was leaning against the counter, its door inaccessible. She struggled to right it, but it was much too heavy. She needed help.

She went to the townhouses neighboring hers. They seemed to have survived except for some fallen chimneys. But no one was home. She moved onto an apartment house on the other side of the street, ringing the buzzer of a couple she knew well enough to greet when they crossed paths. The wife, whose name was Claire, came down to open the door, and Nicole explained her problem.

"Jack just got back from his office," Claire said. "We'll be glad to help. Wait here."

The three of them managed to push the refrigerator to a standing position. Nicole offered them room-temperature white wine and crackers with peanut butter. The three of them sat around discussing the earthquake and the possibility of an aftershock even greater than the original. Such a thing had never happened in their collective memories. But, after every earthquake of note, news outlets seemed to find joy in warning of the possibility.

When the couple left, Nicole was glad she'd sought them out. Being with other people made her feel calmer and less helpless. As she cleared the refrigerator of spills, broken bottles, and food likely to spoil, she promised herself she'd invite them for dinner when things got back to normal. Then, considering all the yet-to-be-reported casualties, fires, collapsed buildings and freeways, she wondered if that would ever happen.

Chapter Two

AFTERSHOCKS AND SCREAMING SIRENS robbed Nicole of the night's sleep. The sirens were constant, and, while the aftershocks didn't last long, each one set her heart pounding. Lying awake, she couldn't help thinking of Jerry. It was unbelievable he was dead, that he'd chosen to end his life. She'd barely get back to sleep before the next temblor rattled her awake. The electricity was still down in the morning, as was phone service. The aftershocks continued.

One good thing had come from her sleepless night. She'd formulated a plan. She'd get in her car the next morning and drive until she found a working airport, hopefully Las Vegas, certainly Phoenix. From there she'd take a plane to London and join Reinhardt. If she had to wait for a flight, she'd be able to check into a hotel. By a stroke of luck, she'd filled her gas tank the day before the quake. The idea of leaving town made her feel better.

She dressed, ate bread and jam for breakfast, and, headachy without her morning coffee, decided to go for a run. Once outside, she could see this was impossible. The minute she stepped out of the building, she stopped, stunned once again by the collapsed and half-broken buildings, fallen electric wires and telephone poles, the wrecked cars that had been pushed from the street to curbs and sidewalks.

A run was impossible with the smoke and pollution hanging in the air. Sirens and building alarms created an angry chorus while a helicopter circled overhead, producing a roar like a fleet of motorcycles. The noise made her headache worse. Water from broken mains gurgled along the gutter creating huge puddles she had to walk through.

The streets were clogged with emergency vehicles and packed cars that appeared to be heading out of town. A police car, using the sidewalk to bypass the gridlock, blared out a message: "Streets are reserved for emergency vehicles. Parts of the 405, 10, and 101 freeways are down. Go home. You can't leave the city." No one seemed to be listening except Nicole. She understood what this meant. It was impossible to escape Los Angeles. It could be weeks—even months—before the freeways were back in service.

Nicole walked a few blocks until she came to the neighborhood's super-sized supermarket. The store looked different this morning, strangely dark without its usual lights. The windows in front were broken, the doors propped open. People came and went; those walking out were carrying unbagged groceries or pushing carts of goods. She didn't expect to find hot, brewed coffee. All she wanted was a coke or another energy drink to help with her headache. She was surprised, then not surprised to find the shelves were almost empty. She headed for the check stand where several people were lined up. They seemed to be arguing with the store's sole employee, a check-out clerk who appeared to be no more than sixteen.

Nicole listened until the argument fizzled out and the other customers drifted away.

"Are you the only one working today?" she asked the checker.

"Yeah," he said. "Nobody else showed."

When Nicole told him what she was looking for, he shook his head. "I was trying to tell those people. We're out of just about everything." His tone was quarrelsome, as if he expected an argument. "The quake knocked most of the inventory to the floor," he went on. "I started to pick it up, but then customers started grabbing stuff. I tried to get them to line up and pay, but the register wouldn't work. So they just took what they wanted and left. Looters came in last night and got most everything else."

He stopped and seemed to be sizing her up. "Look." His voice softened. "I saved some stuff. Let me check in back. There might be some cola. I got milk. Want that?"

"Yes, please. That would be great."

He disappeared and came back with a half-gallon of milk. After putting it in a bag, he said, "No cola. Sorry."

She thanked him and handed him a ten-dollar bill. He gave a smile as he pocketed it. Once she was out of the store, she checked the milk. It was room temperature and would be sour by that evening.

The air, grown worse while she was inside, now burned her eyes and nose. Though the smoke was heavier, the smell of natural gas had faded since the day before. Some of the buildings she passed were partially burned; some were still smoldering. The sirens that had helped disrupt her sleep must have been from firefighters putting out fires and repairing broken gas lines.

By mid-afternoon, a digital version of *The Los Angeles Times* appeared as if by magic on her iPad. It came through the device's cell connection, which made her grateful she'd opted for that service instead of relying on Wi-Fi.

The Times' lead article was about the earthquake. It had measured 7.8 on the Richter Scale, surging hundreds of times more energy than the atomic bomb dropped on Hiroshima. The paper reported the number of fatalities and injuries, statistics it described as preliminary. At present, there was no way to get an accurate count. Fires were still burning, and search-and-rescue efforts were ongoing, thus counts of dead and injured were incomplete. Even so, the numbers were staggering. Over a thousand dead, an estimated 40,000 in need of emergency medical care, 800 trapped beneath collapsed buildings. The quake had rendered at least 100,000 dwellings unlivable. Experts agreed that the final count would be much higher.

On the positive side, some cell phone service had been restored, but circuits were overloaded. Nicole was still unable to reach Melanie to tell her about Jerry. She didn't want to use an email or text to deliver such terrible news, so that had to wait. She did send out additional messages to Reinhardt and her sister. They hadn't replied to her earlier texts, so she had no idea if they'd been received.

When water started dripping from the top floor of the townhouse, she rushed upstairs. The bathtub was filled with brown, foul-smelling water, and the toilet overflowed when she tried to flush it. All efforts with the toilet plunger came to nothing. Finally, she gave up and walked three blocks to use the toilet at the nearest gas station. It was old and rundown but had somehow escaped damage from the quake.

It was closed, a sign posted: "Sorry. Out of gas." But the bathroom was unlocked. It was impossibly dirty, the smell overwhelming. She braced herself and left as soon as she could, relieved to find hand sanitizer in her purse.

While the streets were filled with cars, the sidewalks were relatively empty except for a few people running from shops and office buildings with bags of merchandise as well as computers and other stolen goods. They ignored Nicole. All they seemed to care about was escaping with their loot.

By the time she reached home, it was noon, and she was exhausted from the bad air and scenes of dystopia. It was unimaginable that Southern California—a collection of mostly prosperous cities—could have been brought down like this.

She'd intended to make herself lunch, then take a nap to make up for her sleepless night. But the smell of sewage killed her appetite. Taking a blanket from the linen closet, she eased herself onto the leather recliner. Once again, she lay awake picturing all the quake-driven tragedies unfolding around her.

Finally, she decided to stop torturing herself and get up. After a quick trip to the gas station, she started to pack. Despite the odds, she still held onto the hope that the roads might be open in the morning. Once the sun had set, the condo was enveloped in darkness. Streetlights were out, and the city's usual night glow was missing. For the first time in memory, she could see the stars.

Nicole lit some candles and sat awhile, thinking about all that had happened. When she began to feel less anxious, she blew out the candles and used a flashlight to find her way upstairs to get her pajamas. Driven out by the smell, she hurried downstairs to spend the night on the recliner. She was exhausted but too wired to sleep. She'd finally dropped off when she was awakened by loud banging. She jumped to her feet, imagining the noise to be the start of another quake. Then she realized someone was pounding on the door. When she touched her watch so its face lit up, it said 4:30 a.m. She had a bad feeling about who her visitor might be and what kind of emergency would have brought them out on this night, at this hour. It couldn't be good news.

It was pitch black both inside and out. She got her flashlight and shone it through the small window in the door. Two people stood on her front step.

"Who is it?" she called out.

One of them held up a badge. "Police. We need to speak to you about Jerry Stevens."

"Of course." Nicole said. "You'll have to wait a minute. I'm not dressed." She ran upstairs and changed into a sweatshirt and jeans before hurrying back to the door.

The two stepped inside. The man—clearly in charge—was medium height and somewhat bulky, which gave his body a square shape. He was perhaps in his late forties, with deep lines on his face that created a permanent scowl. "Ms. Graves," he said. "I'm Detective Joe Martinez. My partner here is Detective Breanna Jones."

As Nicole studied his face, she felt a jolt of recognition and wondered where she'd seen him before.

Jones, his partner, had a smooth, amber complexion and cornrow braids. Her face was devoid of lines, which made her look as if she were in her twenties, but she might have been forty or even fifty.

"We need to take you to the station so we can talk about Mr. Stevens' death," Martinez said.

"Why can't we talk here?" Nicole said.

"The station has working electricity."

"No problem," Nicole said. "I have candles. Have a seat while I get them."

"I'm afraid that won't do," he said. "We need to record the interview."

"Why can't you do that on your phone?"

"This is a murder investigation, ma'am. We have procedures—"

"Murder!" Nicole said. "What are you talking about? That was Jerry's own gun. He shot himself."

The lines in Martinez's face deepened. "The direction of the bullet, gunpowder residue, fingerprints, and other factors tell us he couldn't have shot himself. Now are you going to come with us willingly, or do we have to take you into custody?"

Nicole flashed back to the moment she found Jerry. He'd been lying on his gun. She'd picked it up and tossed it out of the way. She must have left her fingerprints. Was that what he was talking about?

And if he really had been murdered, the last thing she wanted to do was answer Martinez's questions. From her previous brushes with the law, she knew it was a mistake to admit anything to the police.

"I want my lawyer," she said.

Martinez gave his partner a knowing glance, as if Nicole had just confessed to killing Jerry. "That's your right," he said. "But you still have to come with us. Let's go."

Nicole got her coat out of the closet, but stood there long enough to give the detectives a piece of her mind: "Do you mean to tell me that—with the whole city falling down and looters everywhere—the police have enough time and personnel to focus on a death that could turn out to be a suicide?"

Neither detective replied. Instead, Jones looped an arm through Nicole's. Martinez took the other, and they hurried her out the door. Nicole wondered if they really thought she'd try to escape.

Their car, which had blended into the night, turned out to be a black, unmarked SUV. Once Martinez started up, he pulled out a siren, clamped it to the roof, and turned it on. He didn't hesitate to use the sidewalk to bypass obstacles in the road, and they sailed through the streets at a good clip.

They drove by the low-lying brick fortress of Wilshire Station, whipped around the block, and parked in a mostly empty lot. She was led to an interrogation room. They put Nicole on one side of the table, and the detectives sat on the other side. Observing Martinez closely, she was still trying to work out why his face was so familiar.

"Please state your name, address, and date of birth," he said.

This was basic information she'd have to give, even if her lawyer were here, so she answered. After that, the detective recited the Miranda Warning. Then he said, "Do you understand?"

"Yes. I told you before. I want my attorney."

Martinez went on as if he hadn't heard. "Several people told us you had major issues with Mr. Stevens. You weren't on speaking terms, and he owed you a substantial amount of money."

Nicole leaned back in her chair. It was true. Jerry had borrowed from her when the firm started having serious cash flow problems. The money came from an inheritance from a murdered work colleague. She hadn't expected the bequest, nor had she wanted it. It had caused her a great deal of trouble, especially since the money was tainted, proceeds from a widespread blackmailing scheme. She'd vowed she'd never spend it on herself and planned to start a foundation and give it all away. But she'd never found time to set it up. Then, when Jerry experienced his first cash-flow crisis, she'd used some of it to bail him out. By the following month, however, it was clear that the loan had been a mistake. He'd continued to gamble and was losing money at an even faster pace. Soon cash shortages were a monthly occurrence.

By now she'd been silent long enough for Martinez say, "Do you want me to repeat my question?"

"I already told you. I want my attorney. You're supposed to stop asking questions once I say that. And I have a right to a phone call."

"Phone calls are out of the question right now," he said. "We've just had a major earthquake, remember? Look, I knew Stevens. He was a good guy. This murder is an outrage, an affront to human decency. I'm doing the right thing. I don't have to justify myself to you or anyone else."

Only now did Nicole remember where she'd seen him. He'd come to their office several times to see Jerry. The two of them had gone out to lunch together and appeared to be on friendly terms. Perhaps that was why he was so bent on finding the killer.

"My phone call?" she reminded him. "According to the news, some phone service has been restored."

"I don't know anything about that," Martinez said. "If you insist, Jones here will take you to our pay phone, and you can give it a try. Don't blame us if you can't get through."

Detective Jones stood up, but Nicole remained seated. "The paper said cell service had more availability."

"Well, for God's sake!" He was clearly out of patience. "Have you got a cell phone?"

Nicole dug in her purse, pulled out her phone, and looked at it. "It's out of juice."

Jones spoke up for the first time, her voice low and husky. "We don't have all day. Let's find you a phone."

Nicole followed her down a hall to the opposite end of the station. Half a dozen people were in line by a single old-fashioned pay phone.

It took a good half hour before Nicole reached the head of the line. The phone was dirty and ancient-looking. She fed in two quarters and got a busy signal. After the phone disconnected, it returned only one of her quarters. She dug in her purse for another and tried again. The phone responded with the same busy signal. This time it held onto all her coins.

Detective Jones was leaning against the wall, watching. She looked slightly amused.

"I can't get through," Nicole said. "And the phone stole my change."

"Well, then," Jones shrugged. "You're out of luck, aren't you?"

"I have a right to speak to my attorney. You must have a working phone here."

"Not for public use," Jones said dryly. "But we do have public defenders on call. You may have to wait a bit, but you will be able to speak to someone."

"I want my own—"

Instead of listening, the detective headed back toward the interrogation room.

Nicole hurried after her. When she caught up, Jones said. "Look, we've done our best to be accommodating, but we're in the middle of a level-five disaster. What would it hurt to answer a few questions? We could sort things out, and you could go home. Otherwise, we have no choice but to hold you until you reach your lawyer. That could take days. Believe me, the women's detention center is not where you want to be."

Nicole knew how this worked. Police lied. She could answer their questions all day long, but it was no guarantee they'd let her go. Either they had enough evidence to arrest her, or they didn't, and they'd have to release her. "I want my lawyer," she repeated.

Jones took Nicole's arm and walked her back to the interrogation room where Detective Martinez was waiting. "Well," he said. "Did you get in touch with your lawyer?"

"No."

"Do you want a public defender?"

"No."

His tone turned more formal. "Nicole Graves. I'm charging you with the murder of Jerry Stevens."

"Martinez!" Jones's tone sounded as if she didn't approve of what he was doing.

He turned to her and shook his finger. "Jones, I'm warning you! You know nothing. You're here to learn how we conduct a murder investigation."

Jones dropped her head, as if in submission. Nicole saw that she was rolling her eyes, as if she were more annoyed than contrite.

Martinez's words had sent Nicole's thoughts spinning. Was she really being arrested for murder? How could this be happening? Would word of her arrest put the media on her trail again, making this nightmare even worse? She reminded herself that these weren't normal times. The press had much more important things to cover than her arrest, even if it was on a murder charge.

Martinez wandered off, leaving Jones to finish booking her. They went to another room where Nicole's mug shot was taken along with her fingerprints. Once this was done, Jones marched her back to the interrogation room and gestured for her to sit down.

"Good luck." Jones paused to study Nicole's face. She opened her mouth as if to say something, then closed it again and let herself out. There was a click, the sound of the door being locked from the outside.

§

After several hours, a uniformed officer put Nicole on a sheriff's department bus. It was full of women, most of them Latina or Black, except for a few who were dirty and disheveled in a way that made them appear homeless. Some of them were asleep. No one spoke. Nicole had the feeling that for many this wasn't their first arrest.

She expected to be taken to the city's main jail, the dreaded twin towers in downtown Los Angeles. Instead, the bus headed south on city streets through poor neighborhoods in South Los Angeles until it passed a sign welcoming them to the City of Lynnwood. The bus pulled up in front of a brutalist, concrete complex that looked as if it were made of enormous building blocks. What caught her eye was one huge block that had shaken loose and slid—or perhaps rolled—into the street.

The women got off and, without prompting, formed a single line. They waited until a woman in a guard's uniform turned up and led them into a barn-like building that was open on one side where the tumbled block had broken off. It was even colder inside than it was in the open air. Those who'd arrived earlier had taken all the benches. Nicole stood a while, wondering when they'd be formally admitted and led to their cells. As more women arrived, and none were taken away, the place grew more crowded. It was clear that intake wasn't going to happen anytime soon. Nicole gave up and sat on the floor. It was so cold she had to stand up again.

"Come sit here, sweetheart." The woman who'd called out was seated on a bench and had slid over to make room. She was dressed in a low-cut, thigh-riding dress and five-inch heels.

Nicole got up and squeezed into the space.

"Whatcha' in for?" The woman asked.

"Um. I didn't do anything."

The woman laughed. "I like you, sweetheart. We're all here on the same charge: we didn' do nothin'. Well, get ready to wait and wait some more. That's their game. Everythin' is on wait-time. What a joke! The way we hafta' wait all this time just to get locked up." She chuckled. "I'm Elana, by the way. You don't want to say why you're here? That's cool. But what's yer name?"

"I'm Nicole. I don't mind telling you. The police think I murdered someone. But I didn't."

"Murder? A little thing like you? No way."

Nicole nodded. "How about you?"

"Same reason as mos' everyone here—bein' a sex worker."

"You mean they're still bothering with misdemeanors when the whole city has fallen down?"

"Yep," Elana said. "Go figure. They'll keep me a few days, try to get me say who's my pimp—which, by the way, I don' have. After they figure they've punished me enough, they let me go. Harassment. That's what it is. My God—you'd think they got better ways to spend their time with all the looting and robberies goin' on, shoot-em-ups and home-vasions."

They chatted a bit about the earthquake and its aftermath. As time passed, more women arrived, and the noise level rose. At one point, a female guard came in, waved a billy club, and shouted, "Shut up! No talking!"

The room went silent. Nicole, leaning against Elena's warm body, nearly fell asleep. At last, the women started getting up. Nicole followed the others outside—all in a neat line—where they waited once again for someone to take them to the next stop. One of the women close to the front waved Elana over, and Nicole lost sight of her.

Throughout her solitary wait, Nicole's thoughts turned to Jerry. Who would want him dead? On the other hand, who wouldn't? He had a lot of enemies: employees he'd treated badly, those he'd fired, and several who were suing him. Also in the mix were people trying to collect on his gambling debts. And, of course, Melanie might have had reason since Jerry was heavily into drinking, drugs, gambling, other women, and running the detective agency into ruin.

She also wondered who on her firm's staff had told the police about the rows she'd had with Jerry. She liked most of the firm's employees and had assumed the feeling was mutual. Of course, most knew about the feud between her and Jerry.

Out of all possible murder suspects, Nicole regarded herself as having the least motive to kill him. True, they'd had their disputes, even one that had turned physical. But she'd never given up hope that he'd turn things around. It might take rehab to help him sober up, settle his debts, and ask forgiveness from those he'd hurt. If he'd pulled out of his downward slide, he might have reconciled with Melanie and moved back in with her and the twins.

Inside the next building, just as cold as the first, the women were forced to undress and squat down for a flashlight inspection of their undersides. This seemed based on the theory that they might be hiding drugs or what?—weapons?—down there. The process was beyond humiliating. Nicole was outraged and resentful while most of the others seemed to take it in stride. She wondered how they could possibly have adapted to such treatment.

They put their clothes back on and endured another long wait before being taken to the next room. Here, women in khaki uniforms stood by bins of clothing. They gave each prisoner a blue two-piece uniform. Examining hers, Nicole noticed a label that said: "Extra Large."

"Don't they have any smalls?" she whispered to the woman in front of her.

Without turning around, the woman breathed, "No. And don't complain or they'll give you something even bigger. Maybe you can trade when we get to permanent housing."

Nicole passed another bin where a woman dressed in a better-fitting gray uniform—perhaps a trustee—handed her equally oversized underwear: white granny panties and a sports bra that might have fit around her twice. A guard attached an ID bracelet to her wrist. At this point, she and her fellow prisoners changed into their blue uniforms and stuffed their streetwear into laundry bags tagged with a label that matched their wristbands. Jewelry, cell phones, and other valuables had been taken soon after they'd arrived. Finally, she and about forty women were led away from the group and crowded into a small waiting room. There appeared to be no heating system in the complex; each room seemed colder than the last.

By now, patches of dark sky could be seen through high, barred windows. Night had fallen, but no one offered them food or drink. Nicole hadn't eaten since the day before, and her stomach was growling. She didn't know which was worse, the hunger, the cold, or the endless wait. She settled on the floor and, still sitting up, nearly fell asleep.

The better part of an hour passed before they were ushered into yet another room to have X-rays taken. Here they were issued a single, thin blanket. No pillow or sheets. At this point, Nicole's group of forty was winnowed down to a dozen. They were marched into what was called "permanent housing." This was a large room furnished with metal tables and chairs. Cells lined the perimeter, and stairs led to more cells above. Nicole was told that she was assigned to one on the second level.

When she reached it, an enormous woman with wild gray hair and mad eyes was standing in the doorway. For a long moment, she seemed to look through Nicole without seeing her. Then she abruptly stepped aside so Nicole could enter. She glanced at the woman, then— uneasy with her ferocious expression—looked away. Her new roomie reminded her of the mad wife in *Jane Eyre*.

The bottom bunk was covered with newspapers and paper bags, which also took up a good portion of the floor. Nicole climbed to the top bunk. Trying to ignore her growling stomach, she lay down and covered herself with the blanket she'd been given. She'd just closed her eyes when her cellmate came in, and the door clanged shut.

"I don't like people who yap all the time," the woman said. "Keep your mouth shut and we'll get along fine." The bed groaned as she climbed in, accompanied by the rustling of paper bags and the sound of chewing.

Nicole squeezed her eyes shut and prayed for sleep that never came.

The next morning, she felt shaky. She forced herself to get out of bed and go downstairs where the women were being served breakfast of dry scrambled eggs, burnt toast, tiny boxes of cereal, and muddy, lukewarm coffee. There was no milk or sugar. Nicole was so hungry she ate every bit. When she was done, she went back to the cell and fell asleep.

She woke up with her enormous roomie shaking her. "Wake up!" she shouted. "Guard says you gotta visitor."

Nicole followed the guard down the stairs out of the unit. "Is it my lawyer?" she said.

The guard, a head taller than Nicole, scowled down at her. "How would I know?"

Nicole followed along, praying that her visitor was Sue, her lawyer, and she was about to be freed.

Chapter Three

It wasn't Nicole's lawyer waiting to see her in the visitor's center. Instead, Melanie, Jerry's wife, was seated on the other side of the partition. Nicole picked up the phone on her side, and Melanie picked up hers.

"The detectives told me they had someone in custody," Melanie said. "I was blown away when they told me who it was. I know you didn't do it. I told them, but they said they had proof."

Nicole explained about the prints she'd left on the gun and how they came to be there.

"I knew it must be something like that." Melanie was pretty with a soft voice and calm, reassuring manner. When they'd first met, Nicole assumed they'd become good friends. On further acquaintance, she found it impossible to get close to Melanie. She had a way of keeping conversations superficial. If anything of a personal nature came up, she turned cool and changed the subject.

"The police asked if Jerry had enemies," Melanie went on. "I named several people from the office and the ones he'd fired who were suing him. You know how it was. People had turned on him, and for good reason." She paused to look around the room—its dirty walls and smudged plastic partitions. "It must be a nightmare being locked up in a place like this. Is there anything I can do?"

"Actually, there is. I need help reaching my lawyer. But there's only one phone in my section. It hardly works, and we're only given a chance at it once a day. Could you get in touch with her?"

"Sure," Melanie said. "If I can't reach her, I can drive to her office and see her."

"Thanks, but she won't be at her office. The quake hit a little after six. I don't think she even gets up that early. She lives in Pasadena. In ordinary times, you could drive out there. But now, with the freeways down—"

"People were driving there before the freeway was built," Melanie said. "There must be a way by city streets." She pulled a tiny notebook from her purse and took down Sue's cell number, which Nicole knew by heart. "What's her home address?"

Nicole raised her arms in a gesture of helplessness. "I don't have it. They took my phone with all my contacts."

"That's okay. I can look it up. Just give me her name."

"It's Susan M. Price," Nicole said. "She lives on Orange Grove Boulevard. But how can you find her address with the web barely working?" It seemed so hopeless that Nicole felt like crying.

"The internet has been working better since yesterday, but it's slow. You have to be patient and keep at it until you connect." Melanie glanced at her watch. "I'd better get going."

"Thanks, Melanie. You're a lifesaver. How are the twins?"

"The quake really freaked them out. They have hysterics with every aftershock, so that's been hard. I'm lucky to have a live-in nanny who's very good with them. She's taking care of them right now."

Nicole suddenly realized she hadn't offered condolences. "I want you to know how sorry I am for your loss," she said. "I can't imagine what you've been going through."

"Thanks, but I lost him some time ago. I've already done my grieving." Melanie's tone was stiff, as if she were reading prepared remarks. She stood up. "I have to go. I'll come back tomorrow if you're still here." By the time she reached the exit, the guard had returned to take Nicole back to her cell.

She was relieved to find her cellmate gone, along with the paper bags and crumpled newspapers. The woman's silent presence had been menacing, adding to Nicole's anxieties.

Lying on the top bunk, she stared at the little patch of gray sky visible through a high, barred window. When lunch was announced, she went downstairs, but the smell of the gray mystery stew made her feel sick. She was thirsty, though, and managed to down several glasses of the grape-flavored punch served in pitchers on the lunch tables. While the others were stoking away their meal, she returned to her cell and lay down.

Staring at the ceiling, she asked herself who might have killed Jerry. Going over the list, she was shocked there were so many. The next question was why the police had decided to focus on her and her alone.

Toward the end of the afternoon, Nicole was summoned again to the visitors' center. This time it was her lawyer, Sue Price. As usual, she was impeccably dressed in a tailored purple suit that made an interesting contrast to her red curls.

"I'm so sorry you ended up here," Sue said. "I managed to get in touch with the deputy D.A. handling your case. The police arrested you without consulting his office, and they're on very shaky ground. We can challenge it on the basis of insufficient evidence. Since the earthquake, police have been making their own decisions about arrests without consulting the district attorney's office. Another problem is that the courts are barely functioning, and, since it's Sunday, they're closed. That means my hands are tied for the moment. You'll have to stay here until tomorrow when the courts reopen."

Nicole was quiet, thinking how miserable it would be to spend another night in the freezing cell. She had other worries as well. "What if the judge decides there is enough evidence? Will you still be able to get me out? Do they allow bail for accused murderers?"

"In that event—which I doubt will happen—I think I could still get you out. Since the earthquake, crime has exploded, and a good number of jail facilities are so damaged that they can't be used. They have nowhere to lock people up. So they're looking for ways to release all but the most dangerous criminals. And, as far as I can tell, those detectives don't have a case. If it's alright with you, I'll like to stop at your home and pick up something suitable for you to wear to court." When Nicole gave a nod, Sue went on: "Do you have a house key hidden somewhere?"

"I do," Nicole said. "There's a fake rock with a key inside to the right of the front door. There are several rocks. You'll have to sort through them."

"Another thing," Sue said. "Is your place habitable? Will you be able to stay there once you're released?"

"Uh-uh," Nicole said. "The sewage backed up in my tub. The toilets don't work, and I doubt the water is safe to drink."

"You could stay with me, but Melanie said she wants you to be her houseguest. She has a working generator and a guest house at the back of her property. I think you'd be more comfortable there. Melanie—wasn't it her husband who was killed?"

"Yes." Nicole's doubts about Melanie surfaced. Sue was an old friend, and she'd much rather stay with her. She didn't know Melanie that well and wasn't even sure she liked her. But Sue sounded as if she didn't have room or didn't want to give up her privacy. This wasn't something Nicole could ask about and expect an honest answer. Instead, she said, "Staying with Melanie would be fine."

They began discussing the growing count of casualties and destruction the earthquake had left in its wake. After a few minutes, the guard appeared and called Nicole's name.

Watching Sue leave, Nicole felt a wave of hopelessness. She told herself to stop being a baby. If Sue was right, all she had to worry about was one more night in the cell. Most of the other women would be here for weeks, months, even years. Then she remembered what Sue had said. The courts were hoping to release all but the most violent and dangerous prisoners. Didn't that mean most of these women would be released? And what about her? Weren't accused murderers considered violent and dangerous?

When she got back to her cell, additional cots had been moved in, and she had three new roommates. So little floor space remained that she had to squeeze past the newcomers, all lounging on their beds, to climb to her upper bunk. She skipped dinner and lay staring through the window at the dark sky, willing time to pass. At last, the women settled into bed, and the lights went out. All that was left was the long night, breakfast hour, and however long it would take for a guard to put her on the bus headed to court. If Sue was right, she'd be free by the next afternoon, but that was hard to imagine.

§

The night eventually passed, along with the morning meal. Nicole was given the outfit Sue had found at the back of her closet, a retro-style suit in periwinkle blue with an imitation yellow daisy in the buttonhole, way too cheery for the gloomy surroundings. Still, it was a relief to get out of the jail uniform. Wearing her own clothes made her feel halfway human.

Sue was waiting when the bus pulled into the alley alongside the county courthouse. Oddly, the structure appeared untouched by the earthquake. Sue led Nicole inside where the halls were packed with prisoners waiting for their cases to be called.

"The court system is all but crippled," Sue said. "Without computers, they can't issue the daily calendar. The court's records and transactions had been completely digitized. This puts judges, attorneys, and police at a tremendous handicap now. With no computers, they're back to using pen and paper. Prisoners can wait here all day without being called for a hearing. Some have to return to jail for the night and return the next day."

"Is that going to happen to me?" Nicole said.

"Absolutely not. I raised a fuss with the DA's office. Your hearing will be this morning. They're having an issue with the charge against you." Sue smiled. "See? I told you not to worry."

"I'm getting out?"

"I would think so. You, my dear, are in need of a long, hot bath."

"Are you saying I smell?"

"Time in detention will do that."

It wasn't long before a man came out of the door marked "stairs" and called out, "Nicole Graves wanted in courtroom nine-oh-three." The elevators weren't working, so Nicole and Sue had to climb eight flights of stairs to reach the courtroom. Inside, all the seats were pretty much filled with waiting prisoners. Instead of being seated, Nicole was ushered to the stand.

"What do we have here?" the judge said.

A man in his twenties stood up and introduced himself as Deputy D.A. Clyde Vogel. With his deep tan and sun-bleached hair, he looked like a surfer. Perhaps he was. "We decline to file charges in this case, your honor," he said. "The police acted prematurely. There isn't enough evidence for a charge, not even probable cause for Ms. Graves to be held over for a hearing."

The judge said, "Case dismissed," and pounded his gavel.

Nicole stood there a very long moment, unable to take in what was happening.

The judge smiled at her. "You may go, Ms. Graves. We have other cases to hear."

Nicole followed Sue out of the room. "Am I free to leave now?"

"Not quite," Sue said. "You have to go back to detention, get your personal belongings, and wait to be formally released. It will take an hour or so. What about Melanie's invitation for you to stay with her? Are you okay with it? What do you say?"

Nicole still wasn't sure how she felt. "Sure," she said. "Fine."

Sue was quick to read her mood. "You sound tentative. If you'd rather stay with me, that's fine. But think of what's going on with poor Melanie. She's in mourning and doesn't seem to have a lot of friends. I think she needs company. Besides, her generator, phone, and internet seem to be working, at least most of the time. I really think you'll be more comfortable there, and you'll have some privacy. My place isn't—"

"No, no. It's fine." Nicole did her best to feign enthusiasm. "Absolutely."

§

It was another three hours before Nicole's property was returned and she was released. Melanie waited in the alley in a big SUV. The twins were in their car seats in the back.

"What was it like being in jail?" Melanie said as Nicole climbed into the passenger seat. "I want to hear all about it."

"Sure. But not now. I want to get as far away from this place as possible. And I need a shower."

"Do you mind waiting until we have lunch?" Melanie said. "The food will be ready, and the boys are hungry. After we eat, I'll show you the cottage. You can have a good soak and spend the rest of the day in bed, if you want."

"That sounds wonderful." Nicole turned to look at the little boys she hadn't seen since they were infants. "My God!" she said. "They're the image of—"

Melanie's pained expression made her swallow her words. They remained silent until they reached Hancock Park where they stopped by a sprawling, white-painted brick house behind a tall hedge. As they pulled up to the curb, Melanie hit a remote to open the gate, then drove along the horseshoe driveway to the front.

Nicole helped unload the twins. Once released, they ran for the house. A small woman in a light blue uniform had opened the front door. She squatted down and held out her arms to receive the twins. When they reached her, she ushered them away.

The house had a large, high-ceilinged great room that served as both the living and dining room. The table was set, and two matching highchairs were in place for the toddlers. Chicken sandwiches and a green salad were set out for the women. Chicken chunks, cut fruit, cheerios, and sippy cups were waiting for the little boys. The nanny was soon back, putting them in the highchairs. When she was done, she disappeared into the back of the house.

Nicole nibbled at half a sandwich before pushing the plate away. Exhaustion and anxiety had robbed her of her appetite. When Melanie finished eating, she got to her feet. "I'll show you the cottage. I think you'll like it." She called out, and the nanny arrived in the dining room as the two women headed out the back door.

Nicole did like the cottage. It appeared to be recently built, the interior decorated in stainless-steel modern with touches of bright, primary colors. The open floor plan featured separate areas for cooking/dining and reading/watching TV. A streamlined bathroom at the back was equipped with both a shower and a tub. The bed was in a loft accessed by a ladder.

It was very nice except for the mess—the books, tchotchkes, and other items that had fallen off shelves and out of cupboards during the quake. Melanie started picking things up, and Nicole joined in. It took a good half hour to make a dent in it. At that point, Melanie reached into a wardrobe and pulled out a robe and PJ's. They were big for Nicole but welcome even so. After Melanie went back to the house, Nicole luxuriated in a long shower and settled in bed for an afternoon nap.

§

A knock at the door roused her. It was Melanie, her arms full of clothes. "I know I'm a larger size—especially since the twins—but I'm hoping something here works for you." She handed the clothes to Nicole. "In the next day or two," she went on, "we'll drive to your place so you can pick up your own things. By the way, dinner is in an hour."

"Thanks, but I'll probably sleep through until morning."

"No problem. If you change your mind, I'll bring your meal out to you. Just call me on my cell."

Once she was gone, Nicole fell asleep again. When she opened her eyes, it was dark out, and her watch said 5:00 a.m. She had the feeling something had woken her. And there it was again, a sound she quickly recognized. Someone was rattling the front doorknob. Were they trying to break in? She knew it couldn't be Melanie. She had a key. Besides, what would she be doing here at this hour?

Using a flashlight that had been left on the nightstand, she hurried downstairs and looked around for another way out of the cottage. But there was only the one door in front, with a stranger trying to break in. By now, the rattling had been replaced by a faint metallic clinking.

She looked out the peephole as the noise continued. Someone dressed in dark clothes was leaning against the door. He was bent over, making it impossible to see his face or what he was doing. But it sounded as if he were trying to pick the locks. There were two, a simple doorknob lock and a deadbolt. Whoever was out there didn't seem to be making much progress.

Nicole moved away from the door, grabbed her cell, and retreated to the back of the cottage. The phone rang for a long time before Melanie picked up. "What's going on?" Her voice was almost drowned out by the sound of a crying toddler.

"Someone's trying to break in," Nicole said in a hoarse whisper. "Turn on the house lights and call the police!" After she said this, she realized the police would still be in search-and-rescue mode and busy hunting down looters, home invaders, and other criminals. It wasn't likely they'd come.

When Melanie turned on the lights, the intruder backed away from the door and disappeared from sight. There was crashing of branches, loud rattling as he climbed the fence, and a thud when he dropped to the ground on the other side.

Through the window, Nicole could see Melanie slowly open the sliding glass door and walk out of the house. She was in a long white nightgown, holding a rifle and a screaming toddler. She looked like a frontier woman setting out to protect the homestead.

As Nicole stepped into the cool night air, her reservations about Melanie evaporated. What had she been thinking? Melanie was trying to protect her. She was a good person. But the sight of her carrying a rifle was a bit jarring. Where had she gotten it? Did she even know how to shoot?

"I don't see anyone," Melanie called.

"He ran away—jumped the fence," Nicole said. "He was trying to pick the lock."

"That must have been terrifying. Would you like to sleep in the house?" The little boy had stopped crying and was now resting his head against Melanie's shoulder. She'd loosened her hold on the rifle, allowing it to dangle.

"I would, thanks," Nicole said. "I don't think I'd be able to go back to sleep out here. If you get me some bedding, I'll make up the couch."

"No, no. We have two perfectly good guest rooms. You have your choice."

"Thank you. By the way, where'd you get the rifle?"

Melanie glanced down at it. "It was—um—his."

"Really? I thought he was rabidly anti-gun."

"That was before. He started collecting them a few months ago."

Nicole's thoughts went back to the attempted break-in. "I can't stop thinking about that intruder. Why would he be after me?"

Melanie bristled. "What do you mean? Why would an attempted break-in at my house have anything to do with you? No one even knows you're here."

"Someone might have followed us from the jail," Nicole said, "when you picked me up."

Melanie shot Nicole a look. "You've been through a lot. But so have I. You always had a tendency—" She stopped, rethinking her words. "Please don't try to make this about you."

Nicole was stung. She was certain the intruder had come for her, and she wasn't grandstanding. She tried to make allowances for Melanie, who'd been through a very great deal indeed. At the same time, she was back to wondering if she'd made a mistake when she accepted Melanie's invitation.

CHAPTER FOUR

IT WAS 5:30 A.M. WHEN NICOLE'S PHONE RANG, rousing her from a deep sleep. She turned on the bedside lamp and looked around the unfamiliar room until memories of the day before came flooding back. Her stomach was buzzing with anxiety when she picked up the phone. It was a jolt when she heard the caller say, "Darling, I heard about the earthquake. Are you alright?"

The sound of Reinhardt's voice made her smile. "Well, I lived through it, and I'm relatively okay."

"No injuries?"

"None."

"Thank God. I've been so worried. Listen," he went on, "I'm trying to get a flight back, but your airports are pretty much shut down. I could get passage on a military plane. But unless I have a life-and-death emergency or an urgent diplomatic mission, they're most unwilling to give me a seat. I'll have to stay in London until more flights open up. What's going on with you? Are you at the condo now?"

"No," she said. "I'm staying with—wait, let me tell you what's happened." She began explaining about Jerry's murder and her arrest. She went on for several minutes before realizing the line had gone dead. When she tried a *69 call-back, the phone made a loud, hiccupping busy signal. Whatever that meant, the phone was unable to connect. She had no idea if he'd heard what she'd told him.

She lay back on the pillow and thought about Reinhardt, how wonderful it had been to hear his voice. He hadn't been scooped up by MI6 for another assignment, as she'd feared. It might take a few days, a week, or even more, but he'd be home again.

The sun was just rising. Unable to go back to sleep, she got up and, still in her PJs, went downstairs. Melanie was already busy in the kitchen, making breakfast for the twins while they pushed toy trains around on the floor.

"Good morning," Nicole said. "Is the internet up?" After their conflict the previous evening, she wasn't sure that Melanie would even speak to her.

But Melanie seemed to have shaken off her bad mood. "Good question," she said. "Let's go up and have a look." After checking that the little boys had enough toys to keep them busy, she led Nicole back upstairs to a handsome, sizeable office that must have belonged to Jerry. She gestured toward a computer sitting on a cherrywood desk. "There it is. Give it a try."

Nicole went around the desk, sat down, and glanced at the screen. "How do I get in?" she said.

"The password is Melanie—from when we first were—" Melanie sighed and let the thought dangle. After a few beats, she said, "I'll leave you to it," and left.

First, Nicole checked the *Los Angeles Times* website for the latest updates on the earthquake. It was mostly a rehash of the previous days' news. She was scrolling down, about to leave the site when she noticed a story about Jerry's murder.

She was astonished. Of all the things going on in the city—the widespread tragedies, destruction, deaths, and injuries—the *Times* had devoted space to this. Most surprisingly, they'd portrayed Jerry as a prominent Los Angeles figure who headed "the city's leading private investigation firm," which she knew was a wild exaggeration. One of the people interviewed described Jerry as "the private eye to the stars."

But her biggest shock was when she saw her own name and realized her arrest for Jerry's murder was part of the story. It went into previous occasions when she'd been in the news, focusing on the multimillion-dollar bequest that had made her a suspect in her former colleague's murder. It also listed several other occasions she'd been under the media's spotlight. In each case, she'd done nothing wrong except be in the wrong place at the wrong time. But the description of her exploits made her look like a criminal mastermind. Each of her moments in the media's spotlight had been a nightmare. Now the *Times* seemed determined to drag her back into it.

Next, Nicole tried to get into the firm's computer system and its databases, but the computer wouldn't connect. She did find a list of the firm's employees. She pulled a yellow legal notepad from a nearby shelf and noted down contact information for people she knew were harboring grudges against Jerry.

At the top of the list was Anita Woolsey. Anita had accused Jerry of sexual battery at a Christmas party several years before. He fired her when she went public with her charge. Another on the list was James Guthrie. He'd sued Jerry for wrongful termination and harassment, accusing him of using anti-gay epithets in his presence.

In yet another wrongful termination case, an African American woman claimed she was a victim of racial discrimination. She was denied a promotion and, when she complained, was fired despite consistently favorable performance reviews.

Judith Hummel, a secretary, had broken her shoulder after tripping over a tangled phone cord in the office. She tried to file a workers' compensation claim, but Jerry refused to sign off on it. He fired her when she lodged a complaint against him with Workers Comp.

There was RJ Barrett. For several years RJ had been their IT guy. He was a hard worker, a whiz with computers, and valuable to the firm. But he was subject to black moods when he would barely communicate with officemates needing help with their computers. Even worse, he'd blame their problems on them and talk down to them as if they were stupid and incompetent. Predictably, this would make them angry.

Conversely, on good days, he'd waylay fellow workers with motor-mouthed lectures about counter-culture topics they had little interest in—the dark web, heavy metal bands, digital currencies, and drugs. He'd refuse to disengage even when it was obvious the other party was dying to get back to work. Nicole tried to make time for a chat when he approached. But she was grateful she had an office with a door she could close when he went on too long. Despite his personality quirks, he was one of Jerry's favorite employees and, at least in Jerry's eyes, could do no wrong.

RJ's pay, along with everyone else's, had been held up during one of the firm's many cash-flow shortages. Normally, the firm caught up with back pay once funds became available. But Jerry had taken a sudden dislike to RJ and refused to give him a cent of the money owed to him. By refusing back pay, Jerry seemed to think he could get rid of RJ and, at the same time, save money. RJ had other ideas. No dummy, he sued for wage theft and wrongful termination.

Others in the office disliked Jerry, but Nicole doubted any hated him enough to kill him. Of much greater suspicion were several men who'd been sent from Las Vegas to collect on Jerry's gambling debts. She had no clue who they were, but they'd struck real terror in Jerry. Several months before, during a period when he and Nicole were still on relatively good terms, he'd confided that "bill collectors from Vegas" had threatened to kneecap him if he didn't pay up.

Nicole had been incredulous. *Kneecapping* was straight out of 1930s gangster films, no longer in anyone's vocabulary. She'd let out a laugh. "They actually said that?"

Jerry had given her a look. "You think I'm kidding? That's exactly what this guy said, and he meant it. You know what I'm going to do? I'm going to hire a bodyguard." But, like so many other things, he'd let it slide.

After Nicole completed her list, she glanced at the clock. It was 8:00 a.m.—a little early to start calling people. Still, the quake must have turned everyone's life upside down. Phone service was probably still out, so it wouldn't hurt to call and try to leave a message. She was surprised when the first call went through, and even more surprised when someone answered.

Anita Woolsey, the sexual battery victim, was already up and in a foul mood. When Nicole told her about Jerry's death, she said, "He totally deserved it," and, "I didn't kill him, I only wish I'd had the satisfaction," and, "Whoever shot him should get a medal." And so on.

My God, Nicole thought. *Anita was lucky the police hadn't questioned her, or she'd be on their suspect list, too.*

After Anita, Nicole called RJ. He answered with a curt "Yes?" as if certain the caller was a bill collector or someone else he didn't want to hear from. When Nicole identified herself, he changed his tone. "Hey,

Nicole! I'm glad you called. I was just thinking I ought to get in touch and see how you're doing."

"I'm okay," she said. "I called in case you haven't heard about Jerry—"

"What happened?"

"Jerry died," she said.

"What? Oh, no—I can't believe it. I mean, how did it happen?"

"He was shot," she said. "At first it looked like suicide, but the police decided it was murder."

"My God!" he said. "Do they have any suspects? Have they arrested anyone?" He sniffled and his voice sounded nasal, as if he had a cold.

"At the moment, I'm their prime suspect," she said. "But I didn't do it—"

"Of course not. But if they thought it was suicide, how did they come up with murder? I mean—who would want to kill him? And how could they investigate it properly when they've got to be overwhelmed right now?" He was talking too fast, stumbling over his words.

After Nicole explained, RJ said, "You mean they're not looking at anybody else?"

"Not as far as I know."

"You know, I've spent some time following Jerry. I mean, before the quake. I didn't mean him any harm. I just wanted to see what he was up to—you know, for my case. I uncovered some interesting stuff. I documented everything. Maybe it could help identify his killer."

"Really? What did you find out?"

"Not on the phone. You can't tell who might be listening. How about you come to my place? Here's the address . . ."

"Wait!" Nicole interrupted him. "I don't have a car." There was something about RJ that made her wary of being alone with him in his apartment. He'd never hit on her or been the least bit flirtatious. It wasn't that. But in his worst moods he seemed dangerous, as if one wrong word could tip him over the edge.

"I'm staying with Jerry's wife, so I can't invite you here," she went on. "Can we meet somewhere near me?" There was a pause while she tried to think of a location. "How about the park by the La Brea Tar Pits. We can meet at the entrance on Wilshire."

"Sure. I'll be there at two." He hung up without waiting for her to confirm the time.

RJ remained on her mind as she tried to reach others on her list. Could he possibly be the killer? He'd spent a lot of time this past year pursuing his case against Jerry and seemed to truly hate him. It wasn't hard to imagine RJ turning violent, and the more she thought about it, the more possible it seemed.

She shifted her focus to the next step, finding out the identity of the debt collectors from Las Vegas. The firm saved videos from the office's surveillance cameras. Under ordinary circumstances, they could be easily viewed on an offsite computer. If she could get access to them, she might be able to locate the men's visit and get a look at them. With near-universal access to advanced facial recognition technology, she could find out who they were. This stopped her. Were the sites available to the public as accurate as databases used by law enforcement? She forced herself to slow down. Letting her thoughts race ahead was a mistake. It made any problem seem insurmountable. Best to limit herself. One step at a time.

She decided to give up on Jerry's computer. It was useless until it could connect with the office and let her look at the security tapes. She glanced at her watch. It was 9:30 and she wasn't dressed yet. Before leaving his office, she took a few minutes to poke through the desk drawers looking for something that might be of use. When she found the bottom left drawer locked, she searched the other drawers until she found the key. The locked drawer contained one thing, a small wooden box hand-painted with morning glories. Inside was a thumb drive. She dropped it in her purse so she could check it out later.

She went back to her room and tried on the clothes Melanie had lent her. Everything was too big. Nicole chose an outfit that didn't look too ridiculous—a denim dress that almost reached her ankles and a red cardigan that might pass as intentionally oversized.

When she returned to the kitchen, the twins had finished eating and were on the floor again, this time playing with blocks. Melanie was cleaning up from breakfast. "Wow!" she said when she saw Nicole's outfit. "Looks like you're playing dress-up in your mother's clothes. We've got to go to your place and get your things."

"Great," Nicole said. "That means I can pick up my iPad."

They left the twins with the nanny and headed for Nicole's condo at 11:00 a.m. On the way, they passed more scenes of devastation—collapsed buildings, fallen telephone poles, wrecked cars. There seemed to be several on every block. One scene was especially poignant. An old apartment building, perhaps five or six stories high, was now a heap of bricks mixed with rubble. Circling it were a number of parked vehicles. A small crowd of people, some crying, were watching search-and-rescue teams digging in the wreckage. Firefighters and what looked like volunteers had come to rescue the living. But five sheet-covered bodies on gurneys were waiting for a ride to the morgue. Unable to tear her eyes away, Nicole stared out the rear window until the scene disappeared from view.

They reached Nicole's townhouse to find a sign posted in front: "Danger. Unstable structure." Below this, a second sign—red and white with a stop-hand symbol—said, "DO NOT ENTER."

They sat for a bit, considering what to do. Finally, Nicole said, "My lawyer was here yesterday and picked up clothes for me to wear to court. I'll bet that sign was already here, and she ignored it. I'll look in the window. If it looks safe, I'll go in."

Melanie was immediately on edge. "What if the building collapses while you're in there? You'll be killed. Besides, you don't need your iPad. You're perfectly welcome to use Jerry's computer. It has the same software you do."

"Mine has my contacts, messages, email—lots of personal stuff. And I really need my clothes. Don't worry. I'll be out in a minute. This isn't a big deal."

"Fine." Melanie hissed. "I'll call 911 when the building falls and crushes you."

Nicole didn't think this merited an answer. She got out of the car, crossed the lawn, and peeked into the front window. The ceiling, floor, and walls all appeared to be at the right angles.

When she walked in, the structure didn't shake or wobble. But items the earthquake had knocked to the floor had been rearranged since she was last here. It looked as if someone had broken in, gone through the fallen objects, and tossed them into untidy piles. Nicole did a double take. Could this be the same person who'd tried to break into the cottage the previous night?

She passed through the living room and started up the stairs to the kitchen-dining room on the next level. She was halfway up when the house started to shake. She stood still, holding her breath and praying it was only a mild aftershock. As the movement grew stronger, she put her arms out to brace herself against the wall on either side. After a few heart-stopping jolts, it wound down.

When it stopped, Nicole thought of her iPad and computer. She'd left them in her office on the top level. Were they the reason for the break-in? Had the intruder taken them? She hurried up to the next level. At the top of the stairs, she froze. The wall safe in the dining room, normally hidden behind a credenza, was exposed, its door yawning open. This was where she kept her few pieces of valuable jewelry and a silver tea set that had belonged to her mother. She rushed over to look in the safe. It was empty.

The credenza—which had somehow stayed in place during the quake—was now in the middle of the room. Scratches on the wood floor showed where it had been dragged. She started looking around. Parts of the tea set and pieces of jewelry were scattered among the piles of detritus. She gathered them up and, assuring herself that most of the pieces were there, put them back in the safe and locked it. It took all her strength to shove the credenza back into place.

On the top level, the bedroom and her small office were similarly disturbed. Art, framed photos, shards of glass, broken table lamps, vases, and the like had been tossed into piles. Just as she'd feared, her computer and iPad weren't where she'd left them. The small filing cabinet was open, emptied of her papers. Most had pertained to personal matters: legal documents, receipts, medical records, and the like. She couldn't imagine why anyone, except herself and perhaps Reinhardt, would find them of interest. She sorted through things on the floor and, to her great relief, found her iPad half hidden in one of the piles. It was in its carrying case. Perhaps the intruder had failed to realize that it held an electronic device with her personal information.

This break-in wasn't like plain, garden-variety looting. They hadn't taken anything of value, just her computer and personal documents.

She was pretty sure this was related to the attempted break-in at Melanie's. Did someone imagine she had information that could put them in danger or implicate them in Jerry's murder? She contemplated this as she threw lingerie and shoes in a tote, grabbed an armful of clothes from the closet, and rushed out of the house. By the time she reached the car, she'd decided not to mention the break-in to Melanie. It would only stir her up again.

Back at the house, Nicole went up to get her jacket and, after explaining to Melanie where she was going, started the long trek to meet RJ.

As she walked, she took in all the fallen trees and telephone poles; the huge potholes and rips in the asphalt; the houses that had burned, been pulled apart, jumped off their foundations, or been battered by fallen trees; cars—crushed, upside down, or abandoned. It bothered her that this no longer upset her. She'd grown used to the destruction. It now seemed almost normal.

Only after she'd gone several more blocks did she notice the silence. It was eerie. There were no people around, no evidence of life. Except for an occasional passing car, she was alone. It was as if the rapture had come and gone, and she'd been overlooked.

At a time like this, wouldn't people be sitting on lawn chairs in their front yards? Where had they gone? Had they left town? Were they killed by the quake? Were they in their homes, hiding from looters and home invaders? But even the looters she'd seen the day after the quake seemed to have disappeared.

She walked a mile and a half, passing block after block of hellscape. Finally, she reached Wilshire Boulevard, and traffic picked up. A few people were out with shopping carts—empty she noticed—and several homeless were snoozing on transit benches.

At last, she reached the tar pits and looked around for RJ. She had to wait only a few minutes before he arrived noisily on a motorcycle. He hopped off and seemed pleased to see her, although his smile turned down at the corners. It was hard to tell if it reflected some other emotion.

RJ was in need of a shave and a haircut. He was neither handsome nor ugly but something about his face seemed to put people at ease, at least until he started talking about his peculiar interests or sucked the air out of the room with one of his phenomenally bad moods.

He was wearing a sizable backpack, which he took off and set on the bench. He sat down next to it. "Here are the photos," he said. "Take a look and see what you think." He placed six photos in her lap, one at a time. They all showed young women wearing very high heels and skimpy outfits showing lots of cleavage, midriff, and thigh.

Nicole picked them up and studied each one. The young women appeared to be in the sex trade, although they were young enough that their clothing style might have been a fashion choice unrelated to their occupation. They were going in or out of a rundown apartment building.

"And these show—?" she said.

"Teenage sex workers!" he said. "Like underage. They're staying in an apartment where Jerry was spending a lot of time. He may even have paid the rent."

She gave him a questioning look. "But Jerry isn't in these photos."

"Oh, I saw him alright. Followed him there a number of times. He'd talk to one of the girls, and they'd go inside. He'd stay for hours."

Somehow, Nicole couldn't picture Jerry in this scenario. It made her wonder if RJ might be mistaken. On the other hand, it was possible Jerry had met with prostitutes even though it was shabby behavior as well as illegal. "Look, RJ," she said. "You haven't any evidence that connects Jerry to these young women or proof they were prostitutes."

"Yeah. I know. I figured I could always follow him again and take more pictures. I guess it's too late now. But think what it means. He corrupted these underage girls, probably wrecked their lives. That would give them a motive for murder! I wish I'd told the police while he was still alive. That would have fixed him."

"I think someone did fix him. Can I ask you a favor? Do you know how to get into the office security tapes? Some men from Las Vegas visited Jerry a few months ago. They were trying to collect on his gambling debts, and they threatened him with violence. They might be his killers. I was hoping you'd help me. If we could find these men and identify them, we might be able to solve Jerry's murder."

He looked away and seemed to disengage. She had the feeling that her failure to show interest in his theory about the girls had disappointed him and put him off.

Finally, he looked at her. "I don't know if it's possible. I mean because of the quake—all the damage it caused probably ruined those tapes."

"Please think about it. If anyone can do it, it's you. And, about Jerry's murder. You really should call the detective investigating it and talk to him. He'll be interested in what you found out. His number is—"

"The police?" he said. "No way! I can't get involved. I have my own problems with them." All at once he was on his feet, pulling his backpack on. He got on the motorcycle, then stood for a moment. "Sorry, Nicole. Wish I could help. Good luck!" He took off, using the sidewalk, and sped around the corner. He was soon out of sight.

§

After the long walk back, Nicole arrived at Melanie's and let herself in. She shouted "Hello!" and got low retort, warning her that the twins were napping, echoed by toddler's wails at being awakened.

"You did it again!" Melanie yelled. "Now they'll be cranky the rest of the day!"

"Sorry!" Nicole hurried upstairs. She got out her iPad and looked at her messages again. She'd heard from Reinhardt but was still hoping for a message from her sister Stephanie. Instead, she found one from RJ. "Good seeing you. On second thought, I think I know a backdoor to office security. I'm going to check it out. Later."

She was about to message him back when she heard the doorbell ring and Melanie greeting visitors. After a moment, she called up the stairs. "Nicole! It's the police. They want to talk to you."

Nicole stood still, trying to figure out why they'd come. Perhaps they'd found more proof and were here to take her in again. No way was she going back to jail. She itched to bolt down the back stairs and run. But what if she was wrong? It was possible they simply wanted to ask her about other potential suspects. In that case, running away would be a terrible mistake.

Then she remembered the altercation she'd had with Jerry. When Martinez and Jones arrested her, they didn't seem to know about it.

But the whole staff had witnessed it. If the detectives had asked around, someone was sure to have mentioned it. Was that enough proof for a new arrest? She had no idea.

Her mind was racing as she tried to figure out what to do. She thought it was highly likely that they were here to rearrest her. Running from the police was something lawyers warned against, and the detectives would be angry if she escaped. But, given the quake's aftermath, they were probably too stretched to mount much of a manhunt. That may have been why they hadn't bothered searching for other suspects.

By the time Melanie shouted out again, Nicole had made a decision. "I'll be down in a minute," she called. "I have to change." She grabbed her purse, jacket, and iPad and tiptoed down the back stairs. Once outside, she ran through the backyard, scaled the rear fence, and raced down the alley. She ran until she couldn't run anymore, then stopped in the front yard of a ramshackle house.

It was already late afternoon, the light dimming. She looked in the direction she'd come from. A car turned onto the street a few blocks away. It was a black-and-white patrol car. As she watched, it turned on its siren and headed toward her.

CHAPTER FIVE

AS THE POLICE CAR DREW NEARER, Nicole looked desperately around for a place to hide. The weeds and low-lying shrubs in the yard of the neglected house were too sparce to offer much coverage. She sank to her hands and knees, so she was at least partially hidden by the foliage, and crawled through the yard as fast as she could. Meanwhile, the siren grew louder. She'd turned her head and was watching the squad car pull up to the curb when she bumped into a tall fence covered with ivy. It separated the yard from the property next door. That yard was so overgrown it was impossible to see the house or if there even was one. With the police nearby she didn't dare try to climb over the fence. Instead, she reversed course and hurried back to the first house.

A basement window was broken and half gone. Pulling out as much of the remaining glass as she could, she wriggled inside and dropped to the floor, painfully twisting her ankle. She forced herself to her feet and limped toward a giant, old-fashioned furnace. Above, car doors banged shut. Moments later, a door slammed, signaling that the police were inside, searching for her. She squeezed into the dark shadows behind the furnace and held her breath.

"I found her!" The voice sounded as if its owner was on the floor above.

"Where?" said someone else.

"In the kitchen."

Nicole peeked out at her surroundings to double check her location. She certainly wasn't in the kitchen.

"Aw, it's not her," came the first voice again. "Just some homeless old drunk."

"I'm not drunk," a gravelly voice protested. "Hey, stop hitting me!"

"That's what you get for assaulting a policeman."

The man protested: "Assault you! You're assaulting me! I didn't do nothing."

"Oh yeah? For one thing, you're trespassing. . ."

"Stop hitting me!" This time it was a shriek.

"That does it. You're coming with us." From above came the sound of them dragging the unwilling stranger out of the house. The noise was punctuated by the man's pleas for them to stop hitting him. Before long, the car drove away.

Nicole felt sorry for the man. On the other hand, she couldn't believe her luck. He'd thrown the police off her track. She looked around for her purse, surprised to find it still slung over her shoulder. She pulled it off and scrambled around for her phone. Failing to find it, she turned the bag upside down and dumped out its contents. It wasn't there. Only then did she remember seeing it on Jerry's desk. She must have left it there.

This presented a major problem. How could she find someone willing to help without a way to communicate? If only she could walk the few blocks to Wilshire where a convenience shop might be open, and she'd be able to buy a disposable phone. But Wilshire was one of the city's best-traveled boulevards, and she didn't dare risk being seen there.

After checking both ways for the police, she left the house and hurried along the quiet lane. Her ankle still hurt, but the pain was manageable. She was east of Hancock Park. The homes here were modest, some in a tumble-down state that appeared to predate the earthquake. Others, crushed by trees or telephone poles or flattened by the prolonged shaking, were clearly its victims. She'd been hoping to ring a doorbell and ask to use a phone, but none of the houses appeared to be occupied.

Too tired to keep walking, she found herself in front of a cottage with a well-tended garden. Part of the roof had caved in, victim of a fallen jacaranda. She walked up to the door and rang the bell. When no one answered, she went around back. The door was standing open. She stuck her head inside and called out. Getting no response, she went in.

She walked through the laundry room into the kitchen where the open cupboards revealed empty shelves. Their contents—dented cans, broken jars, smashed boxes of cereal, and their spilled contents—were lying on the floor. A pot with two broken eggs lay in front of the stove along with a dented percolator crusted with dry coffee grounds. It looked as if someone had been making breakfast when the quake hit. They must have fled and, for whatever reason, hadn't returned.

The breakfast room was next, where an old-fashioned rotary phone was attached to the wall. She picked it up, surprised to get a dial tone. Then she paused, trying to think of who she could call for help. Joanne, her close friend from the office, came to mind. Nicole knew her phone number and placed the call.

On the third ring, Joanne picked up. "Nicole! I thought the phones were still down. Are you alright?"

"I'm okay, but I need a favor."

"Of course," Joanne said. "Anything."

"Just a sec," Nicole let the phone dangle while she stepped to the window and checked outside to be sure there were no police cars around. When she picked up the receiver again, she said, "Things have gotten hot for me since Jerry's death," she said.

"I know," Joanne said. "I saw the article in the *Times*."

"Right. That means I have to hide until I can prove I didn't kill him."

"Of course you didn't kill him. Come stay with me. Do you want me to pick you up?"

"That would be great. But I have to warn you. If you do that, you'll be opening yourself to the charge of aiding and abetting or accessory to murder after the fact. I'll understand if you say no."

"Don't be ridiculous. You're, like, my best friend. Where are you?"

"Oh, God. Thanks. I'll get you the address. Hang on." She went to the front door and down the steps to look at the street number.

When she reported it back, Joanne said, "I know exactly where that is. I'm not far away. I'll pick you up in, say, ten minutes."

Joanne arrived in her ancient Volkswagen in less than five.

"Can I borrow your phone?" Nicole said as she buckled herself in. "I need to call my lawyer."

"Sorry," Joanne said. "I was in such a rush that I left it home." She reached into the rear seat, then handed Nicole a jacket with a hood. Nicole put it on and pulled up the hood to cover as much of her face as possible.

Joanne's house was a classic California bungalow in the center of a tree-covered lot. The dry leaves crunched as they walked up the path.

As soon as they were inside, Joanne reached into the drawer of a cabinet and pulled out a burner phone. "This is a spare," she said. "I bought it a few weeks ago when I couldn't find my cell. Why don't you take it. You can make your call while I fix something to eat."

Nicole put a call in to Sue, who picked up immediately and spoke in a rush, "I'm expecting a call from a criminal defense attorney I contacted on your behalf. I'll call you back." With that she disconnected.

Nicole was stunned. Sue had hung up so abruptly, she hadn't had a chance to give her the number of the burner phone. She tried to call Sue back, but her line was busy. Frustrated, she hung up.

She was headed for the kitchen when she spotted Joanne's paperweight and snow globe collection, usually on display in her office. They were now sitting on the dining room table along with her desk pen, mousepad, and laptop.

When Nicole walked into the kitchen, Joanne was busy stirring something in a large pot. "Your things from the office are here," Nicole said. "You must have been there since the earthquake."

Joanne nodded. "I went in yesterday to get my stuff. You ought to do the same. Looters have broken into several offices in the building."

"After the quake, a paramedic told me the building wasn't safe."

Joanne shrugged. "It seems okay now. There's no warning sign in front, and other people were dropping by to get their things."

"Who else was there?"

"Let me think," Joanne said. "Nate Goodwin. He seems to think he's in charge."

Nicole shook her head. "I wonder where he got that idea. Given that I'm out of the picture, it should be Melanie."

"Right," Joanne said. "I also saw Mary, Hank, and Elizabeth. Everyone was gobsmacked by Jerry's death, and they seemed uneasy. Like they're afraid the police might come after them." She paused, then her eyes lit up. "Oh—you'll never guess who else was there. RJ. He hasn't worked for the firm in at least a year, but there he was, using Tad's computer. I pointed this out to Nate, but he shrugged it off. Now that I think about it, the whole encounter was kind of strange—the way people were acting."

Nicole nodded. "Sounds like it. I want to go down there and get my things. But I think I'll wait until tonight, so I don't run into anyone. Would you mind if I borrow your computer for a bit?"

"Have at it," Joanne said. "But first, I'm wondering. Why did you run from the police if you're innocent?" Before Nicole could reply, Joanne went on. "Never mind. You don't need to explain. I'm sure you had your reasons. Follow me." She led Nicole to a makeshift office in her bedroom, typed in the password to her computer, and headed for the kitchen. "I'll call you when lunch is ready."

Nicole got out the thumb drive she'd taken from Jerry's desk. She'd wondered if anything was on it. Now she had the time and means to take a look. Sure enough, the drive held two file folders. She opened the first one, and a series of text messages came into view. It turned out to be an email exchange between Jerry and an unknown party who signed his messages GuessWho. The second folder contained emails from someone whose email ID was Juiceman. Jerry must have copied these files from his office computer. Perhaps he'd deleted the originals and brought the copies home to prevent anyone from finding them.

In GuessWho's first message, they claimed to be Jerry's unacknowledged child. Whoever the sender was, they chose not to reveal any clue to their identity or even their gender. The message read:

> Think back to a starry night in June while you were a student at UCLA. You took an innocent fifteen-year-old girl up to Mulholland Drive to look at the moon. Instead of enjoying the view, you raped her. Do you remember?
>
> What about when she appeared at your dorm to tell you she was pregnant and needed money for an abortion? You and your buddies laughed and walked away.

Maybe you've forgotten this chapter in your life. Well, I'm the twenty-year-old product of that fateful night, and I've come to remind you.

What you may not realize is that we already know each other. We're in contact almost every day. You'll never guess who I am. The girl at the Starbucks where you get your morning mocha latte? The postal carrier who delivers the mail to you on the eighth floor of Wilshire Tower? The shoeshine you pass on your way to work? Wouldn't it be amusing if I turned out to be the latest hire in your office?

I'm not asking to meet you, although you might find it interesting. All I want is payment for what we went through when you abandoned us. She told you she was pregnant and contacted you many times while I was growing up to ask for child support. You never answered. She died three years ago after a long illness. I blame you for her death.

You owe me. Now that I've found you, I intend to collect—one way or another.

Nicole stared at the email, taking in its malevolence. Looking at Jerry's reply, she found it consistent with the man she knew. Even at his best, he was heavily into denial. "You've got the wrong guy," he wrote. "Stop bothering me."

After that, at least a dozen emails from GuessWho were in the file, although it didn't include any responses Jerry might have made. For the most part, they were a repeat of the first message with the threats amped up: "You'd better watch your back" and that old saw, "You can run but you can't hide."

Nicole had a feeling that GuessWho was most likely a man, and his messages sounded both ominous and fake. Would a twenty-year-old be that articulate? Possibly, but GuessWho sounded more mature than someone barely out of his teens. His threats would have been more believable, she thought, if he'd wanted to meet his lost parent, no matter how much he hated Daddy and lusted for revenge.

She looked at the second folder on the drive. This one contained quite a few messages from someone calling himself Juiceman. Most were friendly in tone, suggesting they go to a ballgame together or meet for lunch. The last message, however, contained a threat. It demanded Jerry pay back $250,000 he'd borrowed. "I arranged that loan," Juiceman said. "When you didn't make your payments, and they tried to collect, you told them to get lost. That leaves me holding the bag. No way I'm letting this happen. Pay it back. Every cent." Jerry didn't seem to have replied, or if he had, his response wasn't on the drive.

Nicole wasn't quite as surprised by the second string of messages as she was by the first. She'd long known that Jerry owed money, that his compulsive gambling was the source of his troubles. But the amount of his debt shocked her. He'd complained to her about creditors from Las Vegas who'd threatened him. Apparently, Juiceman had arranged a $250,000 loan. But who was the creditor? Was it the same party who'd sent the Las Vegas contingent? Or was this amount in addition to that debt?

She had to get the police to read these emails and take them seriously. But how? It took only a moment for her to figure it out. The media. She could use it to get the police to pay attention.

From her own time in the headlines, she knew an *L.A. Times* reporter, Greg Albee, who'd turned one of her earlier cases into an investigative piece that had all but blown the roof off city hall. She hadn't seen Albee's byline in a long time and wondered if he was still at the paper. After looking up his phone number, she gave him a call. A recorded voice told her his number was no longer in service. This was disturbing. Had he moved on or had something happened to him?

She was disappointed she couldn't reach out to him, but she knew the paper had a way for people to leave information anonymously. She found the paper's contact list and clicked on the icon for their tip line. A page came up with the words: *Got a tip?* It provided three ways to leave a tip or leak for the paper: on their secure messaging app, with an encrypted email, or through the U.S. Postal Service.

She decided that the messaging app would be the fastest and most direct method. After taking screenshots of the emails from GuessWho and Juiceman, she dragged them into the blank space on the website that said, "add photos or images." Next, she wrote a brief note explaining that they were taken from a thumb drive belonging to Jerry Stevens, the murder victim, and that they might lead to his killer.

After sending in the tip, Nicole began to worry that it might go nowhere. Only by a stroke of luck would the information be given to someone who'd actually write a story. Odds were that it would be read by a copy messenger or intern who'd never heard of Jerry or his murder. In that case, her tip was likely to end up in the trash.

She got up from the computer feeling deflated, itching to return to an earlier version of her life when she could appear in public without fear. She was no longer in jail but was now a different kind of prisoner, cut off from most everyone and everything. She daydreamed about escaping to Mexico, how nice it would be to catch a flight there. From the airport in Tijuana, she could fly to London and reunite with Reinhardt. Of course, that was impossible. First of all, she couldn't risk using a credit card to buy an airline ticket. And, even if she could clear that hurdle and had her passport with her—which she didn't—the effort would land her back in jail. The moment she showed the passport at airport security, TSA would be alerted that she was wanted by the police. Airport security would hold her until cops arrived and took her into custody.

A little after 10:00 p.m. she borrowed Joanne's car and set out for the office. Just as she'd hoped, the lights were out, the building dark and apparently deserted. She parked in the alley behind the building and used a flashlight Joanne had lent her to find her way upstairs. Yellow crime-scene tape was hanging on one side of the entrance, evidently pulled aside by her coworkers.

Nicole hadn't come to retrieve her belongings as she'd told Joanne. Instead, she planned to copy files from her computer and look for more information on Jerry's computer—if the police hadn't hauled it away. For that purpose, she'd brought along the thumb drive from Jerry's office. There was still plenty of room on it.

On her way down the hall to her office, she noticed a nasty smell—sharp and unpleasantly sweet. It was somehow familiar, although she couldn't place it. Perhaps it was the chemicals the forensics team had used when they examined the murder scene.

She planned to make a quick exit. But first she went right to her office and logged into her computer. She copied her contact list, email, and messages onto the drive. This took just a few minutes. She considered trying to get a look at the security tapes to see if she could find the thugs from Las Vegas, but decided it would take too long.

She got up and hurried down the hall to Jerry's office to see if his computer was still there. The odor she'd noticed before grew stronger as she approached his door.

When Nicole opened it, the smell was unmistakable. It was blood—blood that had been left to ripen a while. She turned on her flashlight and swept the room with its beam. There was something lying on the floor near the desk. Hair rose on the back of her neck as she approached it. Just as she feared, it was a body. As soon as she was close enough, she focused the flashlight on its face and rocked back on her heels. It was Diana Chang, the young woman who'd arrived with Nate Goodman when Jerry was bleeding out. From the amount of blood on the floor, it looked as if Diana had bled out hours ago. She'd been shot through the forehead, and she was very dead.

Nicole got out the burner phone, ready to call 911. Only then did she realize that she—of all people—couldn't report Diana's death. Even calling anonymously was out of the question. It might allow the police to track her new phone and learn she'd been at the scene of yet another murder. She also had the feeling that, whether or not they tracked her here, they were still going to blame her for Diana's death.

She was trying to figure out what to do when the beam of a flashlight almost blinded her. She stepped to the side so she could see. Nate was standing in the doorway. He took a few steps forward until his flashlight beam found the body, and he stopped. For a long moment, his mouth moved, but no sound came out. Finally, he moaned, "Oh, my God. She's dead!" He looked at Nicole and said, "Why her? Why would . . ." He didn't finish, but Nicole felt the accusation.

"It wasn't me!" Her voice came out in a whisper. "I found her like this. Look at the blood. Some of it's dry. That means she's been here for hours, maybe overnight."

"Right." His voice quavered. "Sorry. I know you didn't do it. I—I didn't mean—"

"That's alright," she said. "It's a terrible shock to see her like this."

"You know what?" Nate went on. "The morning we found Jerry, she told me something. We'd been clubbing the night before. Well, I guess she wasn't used to drinking because she got pretty drunk. So, she decided to spend the night here rather than driving home. That morning she told me a gunshot woke her up, and she saw someone run away."

"Did she get a close look? Did she recognize who it was?"

"That's the thing! She wouldn't talk about it. I wanted her to go to the police, but she wouldn't. I think she was too scared."

"If the killer knew she'd seen him," Nicole said, "he might have threatened her. I came here tonight hoping to find proof that I didn't kill Jerry. Now, after finding poor Diana, I'd better leave. You need to call 911 and report her death. I can't do it because the police already think I killed Jerry, and they'll blame me for this. Please don't tell them you saw me. They'll probably try to pin this on me anyway. But it would be worse if they knew I was here."

"Okay," Nate's voice trembled.

For the first time, Nicole looked at Jerry's desk and sure enough, a computer was there. She regretted that she didn't have time to look at his files. But she had to leave.

"I'm going," she said. "As soon as I've left, please call 911."

Nate didn't answer or even look up as she hurried out of the room. She was approaching the front door of the suite when she heard familiar voices just outside. It was Martinez and Jones. Nicole ran back down the hall and squeezed into a supply closet, leaving the door open a crack.

Seconds later, the detectives hurried past her hiding place and went into Jerry's office. "Who is this?" Martinez said. "Is she dead?"

"Yes. I—I'm pretty sure," Nate squeaked. "Her name is Diana Chang. She works—used to work here."

"And who are you? What are you doing here?"

"I'm Nate Goodwin. I work here, and I'm filling in as the office manager until things get straightened out. I came down to finish up some work. Then I saw Diana and . . ."

At this point, Martinez interrupted to introduce himself and Jones. "We're investigating your boss's murder and came back to be sure the suspect, Nicole Graves, hadn't returned here. Now, we find this."

"You're putting this on Graves, too?" Jones said.

"You do the math," Martinez snapped. "Same M.O." There was a brief silence, then he said, "Unless it was this guy. You know something? Maybe Graves didn't do it after all."

"Wait a minute!" Nate said. "I just got here! Look at the blood. It's already part dry. This happened hours ago, maybe last night."

"Okay. Do you have an alibi? Can you prove you weren't here last night?"

Nate raised his voice. "I'm telling you; it wasn't me. When I first walked in, Nicole Graves was standing over the body. She left before you arrived."

Hearing this, Nicole was disappointed but not surprised. Nate was afraid they were going to charge him with Diana's murder.

"Now, that's real interesting," Martinez said. "You can tell us all about it when we get to the station. Put your hands behind your back so I can cuff you. That's a good boy."

Nicole understood one thing: No matter what Martinez told Nate about being a suspect, he was still convinced she was the murderer. He was just trying to scare Nate into helping the police build their case against her.

She listened to the sounds of the three of them walking to the front door.

"Wait," Martinez said. "We have to lock up. Jones, call the station and have them send someone to patrol the building. Graves may still be here."

Nicole listened with a sinking heart. She'd left Joanne's car in the alley next to the building. How was she going to get away? She reminded herself she'd been in worse scrapes. At least the people looking for her weren't trying to kill her or throw her into a foreign prison without a trial. Somehow, this wasn't reassuring.

CHAPTER SIX

ONCE THE POLICE WERE GONE, Nicole went back to Jerry's office hoping to copy the rest of his emails. When she trained the beam of her flashlight ahead of her, it caught Diana's body, now covered with the blanket from Jerry's couch. Even though she'd seen it before, she froze. For a moment, she could picture Diana slowly sitting up and rising to her feet. She had to fight the urge to run.

She forced herself to sit down at Jerry's desk and sign into his computer. This time the computer rejected the password. She tried again with no better luck. She looked closely at the images on the screen. The hard drive was labeled "Nate's Machine." That explained it. The police had taken Jerry's computer, and Nate, in promoting himself to top dog, had commandeered Jerry's office and moved in with his own computer.

She got up and, averting her eyes from the body, left the office. As she shut the door, a hopeless feeling swept over her. The drive that had been pushing her along had disappeared. If it were possible, she would have spread out on the carpet and prayed for sleep. But Martinez's last words kept repeating in her head: "Have them send someone to patrol the building. Graves may still be here." Coroner's deputies had been called as well, and they could arrive any time. She had to leave before any of that happened.

The detective agency occupied the whole top floor of Wilshire Tower. Nicole was able to walk from office to office to get a 360-degree view of the surroundings. No vehicles of any kind were in sight. She let herself out of the suite. Tiptoeing down the stairs, she paused on each landing to make sure no one was climbing up from below.

In the lobby, she looked through the tall bank of windows facing the street as a black and white pulled up to the curb. She ducked behind the lobby's marble reception desk, which had fallen on its side. Before the quake, this was where visitors showed their IDs before being allowed access to the offices upstairs.

After a short time, the squad car drove away. She decided to wait and see what would happen next. About ten minutes later, the cruiser reappeared and, just as before, parked briefly before moving on. It appeared to be patrolling the perimeter of the building on a loop. She waited until he repeated the pattern once more. The moment he was out of sight she dashed outside.

She'd just reached a bank of oleander at the edge of the alley when the patrol car pulled up behind her. She slipped into the shadows, but he'd already seen her. He jumped out of his car and gave chase. She ran as fast as she could, but by the end of the alley, he'd almost caught up with her. She hopped down a short stairway that led to the garage of a neighboring high-rise. It appeared to have been damaged by the quake and leaned to one side. From the sound of departing footsteps, she could tell that the cop hadn't seen her detour into the garage.

Once inside, she ran up the ramp and hid between two parked cars. The building seemed to be swaying. She hoped it was her heightened state of awareness and not a sign that the structure was about to collapse.

By now the policeman had turned around and entered the garage. Nicole spotted the glow of his flashlight on the level below. He soon paused, and she heard him put in a call for backup. She tried the doors to several parked cars until she found one that was unlocked. She started to open it, but the car's interior lights went on. After shutting it, she scurried further up the ramp. Apparently the cop hadn't seen the light, but she could hear him methodically making his way toward her. He kept calling out things like: "Give it up. You don't need to run," and, "I'll keep you safe," and, "No one's going to hurt you."

After turning the corner onto the next level, she crawled under a car and lay flat on the pavement. Sirens blared as more cops arrived and joined the search. As they drew nearer, she squeezed out from under the car and ran up two more levels. This time she didn't try to hide in or under a car. The police were getting closer, and she needed to be able to keep running.

She spotted a glowing EXIT sign above the entrance to a stairwell and edged her way over. Ducking between parked cars on her way toward the sign, she reached the stairs and started down. Meanwhile, she kept watch, fairly certain that the cops would soon figure out where she was. She'd almost reached street level when she heard one of them shout: "She's over there—on the stairs."

She'd parked at the end of the alley, just a short distance away. She raced out of the garage to Joanne's car and got in. Without turning on the headlights, she started up, tires screeching as she made a sharp turn onto the street. Seconds later, police sirens started up.

A few blocks away, she spotted an open garage. It was part of a tiny house squeezed between two tall buildings. She drove inside, jumped out, and pulled the door closed.

Sirens blared nearby, then shut off. She stood still, holding her breath. Had they seen her enter the garage, or had they stopped to figure out where she went? Finally, the sirens started up again, growing fainter as the patrol cars drove away. Once it was quiet again, she climbed back in the car to wait until she was sure they weren't coming back. It wasn't long before her sleepless nights caught up with her, and she dozed off.

When Nicole awoke it was early morning and quite chilly. She'd been there all night. She peeked out of the garage. Dawn was just breaking. The neighborhood was ghostly still.

She drove out onto the street and headed for West Hollywood. Turning onto Joanne's street, she came to an abrupt stop. Detective Martinez's car was parked in front of the bungalow.

She backed around the corner to keep watch. Nate must have told the detectives that she and Joanne were friends. They were probably hoping to find her here.

As time passed and the detectives remained inside, Nicole wondered if they were trying the same tactic on Joanne as they had on Nate— threatening her with murder charges to scare her into talking. She couldn't imagine Joanne falling for it. But it was hard to predict what someone might do when faced with the charge of accessory to murder.

Nicole waited until Joanne was marched out of the house by the detectives. Once she was in the back of their SUV, they drove away. Considering what her next step would be, she got out her wallet to see how much money she had. She'd gone to the ATM the day before the quake and still had $300, enough to buy a train ticket out of town.

She decided to drop off a note at Joanne's telling her where she was going to leave the car. She found paper in the car's glove compartment, but no pen. She got out her lipstick and scrawled a note. After making sure no one was around, she pulled up to Joanne's house and dashed out just long enough to shove the note through the letter slot.

Her next stop was Union Station, L.A.'s iconic mashup of Art Deco, Mission Revival, and Streamline Modern architecture. She parked the car in the front lot, where Joanne could easily spot it. She left the parking ticket in the storage on the center console and the keys under the seat. The door of the station was closed and locked. A posted sign announced that the trains were out of service because of damaged tracks and other problems. It directed passengers behind the station where buses were available. She walked the long block to the rear of the building and caught a bus to Pasadena. She got off near Sue's address on Orange Grove Boulevard, otherwise known as Millionaire's Row.

Light from a crescent moon guided her along. Among the landmark mansions lining the street, condo developments had replaced several houses that had been torn down. Sue's place was in a complex with a canopy of magnolia trees. Two of them had toppled and were lying side-by-side on the broad lawn.

Nicole had to knock several times before the door opened. "The police just called to let me know you're a fugitive," Sue said. "As your friend, I want to tell you how disappointed in you I am. I thought you had more common sense. As your attorney, it's my duty to urge you to turn yourself in. I can arrange that."

Sue was completely devoid of her usual warmth. It was as if she were talking to a stranger instead of an old friend. "You're angry I ran away," Nicole said.

"Of course I am!" Sue said. "You've made things so much worse for yourself. If you're eventually tried, the jury will get the murder charge, along with a flight instruction. That means you left to avoid arrest and being charged. This is considered evidence of guilt. I don't know," she added, half to herself. "With everything in chaos—the whole justice system practically shut down—old rules like that may be out the window. Still, it was a very foolish thing to do."

"But I'm a trained investigator, and the real murderer is still out there. The police aren't looking for him. If I'm in jail, there will be no investigation. Surely you can see that."

"Here's the problem," Sue said. "You are the worst possible investigator for your own case. Even if an attorney gets arrested, he doesn't do his own investigation. That's the job of the P.I. working for the defense attorney."

"But I don't have a defense lawyer."

"Well, that door is still open," Sue said, "I have calls out to several qualified attorneys and may yet find someone for you. Meanwhile, unless you're willing to surrender, I can't help you. If I did, I could be charged as an accessory after the fact. That's a felony with a prison sentence. I'd be disbarred. I can't risk it."

"But how would anyone know?"

"That detective went out of his way to tell me you're a fugitive and that he has a warrant for your arrest," Sue said. "Frankly, I don't understand why he's pursuing you with all the other crime going on. Maybe the authorities cut him and his partner loose from other responsibilities to find you, but that doesn't make much sense. Because I'm your lawyer, they probably expect you to turn up here. And that's exactly what you've done. I'm closing the door now. You'd better leave. Good luck."

Before the door clicked shut, Sue whispered, "Meet me out back. Side gate."

Nicole headed around the building and through the gate. The yard—overhung with trees–was pitch dark. Without the usual night glow hanging over the city or light from surrounding buildings or streetlights, she had to feel her way along.

"Over here," came a disembodied whisper. Sue was waiting in the shadows behind the building. "Sorry for the charade at my front door. But the police really might be watching. Do you realize that this case has become high profile? It's top news along with coverage of the quake.

You like to deny the fact that you became a celebrity when several of your cases went viral. But people know who you are. You're the most famous P.I. in the city. That's why the *L.A. Times* is covering your murder charge and flight from the police."

"You know how I hate publicity like that."

"I do, and I think it's foolish. Because of your news coverage, people are interested in what's going on with you. They respect what you've done in the past. When the facts about this murder charge come out, they may be sympathetic. It could work in your favor."

Nicole shrugged. "Press coverage and public opinion are the least of my concerns. Since I'm not turning myself in, what am I supposed to do?"

"I have no idea." Sue was silent for a long moment before adding. "If someone in your situation asked a friend for advice, the friend might say, 'Take a look at all the big, old houses on this street. Many of the owners are wealthy enough to have several homes, and most of these places are occupied part-time, if at all. Right now, there are more vacant houses than ever. People would rather be anywhere else.'"

"Okay," Nicole said. "Got it."

"But that friend would also say that breaking in won't be easy," Sue went on. "Most of these homes have security systems. To get in, a person would have to know how to pick a lock and disable security."

After Nicole thought about it, she said, "The quake knocked out power, phonelines, and cell towers. Wouldn't a lot of home security systems be thrown offline and need to be set up again?"

"Possibly. I'm no expert. I'd better go inside now. If I were you, I really would turn myself in. As I said, I can help you do that."

"I wouldn't be doing myself any good locked up. When they got around to a trial, I might end up spending the rest of my life in prison."

"Well. That's your decision," Sue had turned chilly again. "Good luck."

Nicole came out of the yard and walked along Orange Grove Boulevard, feeling profoundly discouraged. Most of the mansions did look deserted. But how many had working electricity? Up-to-date computers? Wi-Fi? Any one of them, however, might provide a safe place for her to shelter for the night. She was about to head up the path of a house with a telephone pole resting across its lawn, when a car jumped the curb and screeched to a stop in front of her, blocking her path.

Certain it was the police, she was in a full panic until a familiar voice called out. "It's me. Don't run away. I want to help you."

Nicole gave a closer look. It was RJ, driving an ancient black Volvo sedan. "What the—?" she said. "How did you find me?"

"When we met at the park, I dropped a tracking device in your purse. Sorry, but I was worried about you. I followed you back to Jerry's house and picked up your trail again when you went to the office last night. The police chased you, and you drove into that garage to hide. I waited all night to see where you'd go next. And I was behind you when you went to Joanne's—that was her house, wasn't it? Then to Union Station. After you went in, I kept track of you with my phone. That's how I knew you were here. I came because I want to help you find Jerry's killer."

"Okay." Nicole was poking around in her purse for the tracking device. It turned out to be quite small, a disk-shaped device that fit in the palm of her hand. She tossed it on the ground, her mind reeling. This had a science fiction, eye-in-the-sky feel to it.

Once she was seated in the car, she said. "Do you really want to find Jerry's killer? I don't get it. Why do you even care? I thought you hated him and were glad he was dead."

"No," RJ let out a muffled sob, then covered his face with his hands. He tried to speak but was crying so hard she couldn't understand him. Finally, he calmed down. "I never hated him," he said. "I loved him."

Nicole was flabbergasted. "But you said all those terrible things about him. And you followed him, trying to prove how evil he was. I even thought you might have killed him."

"I know, I know." He started crying again. "It was the way he treated me. When he gave me my last performance review, he seemed kind of flirty. I misunderstood and made a pass at him—big mistake. That's when I realized he's—he was homophobic. He called me a filthy perve and fired me on the spot. I was so disappointed and hurt. I couldn't forgive him, but I couldn't get over him either. I'd never have hurt him.

Never. I want to find his killer as much as you do." He wiped his face on his sleeve before correcting himself. "Almost as much.

"Listen," he went on. "I really can help. I have all kinds of computer equipment. We can go back to my place and investigate people you suspect of killing Jerry. And I found a backdoor to get into the office computers. We'll be able to look at those security tapes. Anything you want."

"That's great," she said. "Let's go!"

Once she was onboard, RJ sped off, winding through city streets. Circumventing the closed freeway, he drove through the residential neighborhood surrounding the Hollywood sign. It was no longer standing, a sorry sight with its letters and supports scattered on the ground.

RJ's apartment appeared little affected by the earthquake. Even so, it was a mess; the small living room was cluttered with electronic equipment including at least half a dozen computers.

Nicole handed him the thumb drive. "Look in the first folder. It has a string of messages from someone who calls himself GuessWho. Is it possible to find out who that is?"

RJ sat down in front of a computer and went to work. Once she was seated next to him, she glanced at the clock. It was 5:30 a.m. Her flight from the police felt as if it had been days ago, not hours. It had been a very long night. Even without sleep, she was wide awake and hyperalert, as if she'd had a dozen cups of coffee.

Watching RJ at his computer, she was impressed by the way his fingers flew over the keyboard. "Most of the time it's fairly simple finding out who sent an email," he explained, "You start by opening the message, clicking in the address field, and asking for the raw data." When he demonstrated how this was done, it didn't look simple at all. An incomprehensible string of email addresses and code filled the address field. It was a good ten minutes before he stopped tracking information and turned to her. "His name is Garrick McVeigh. When he set up this address, he was living in Topeka, Kansas. That was a couple of years ago, so he might have moved. You can figure that out from your PI databases, right?"

"I could if I didn't have to use my name to sign into them. But then the police would be able to track me. Please take a look at the other file on the drive. It contains texts from someone who calls himself Juiceman. He might have been a friend of Jerry's, but the last message contained a threat. Can you find out who he is?"

RJ began typing again, faster than before. Once in a while, he took his eyes off the screen—fingers still racing—to glance at the computer on an adjacent table.

"Why do you keep looking at that other computer?" she said.

"Making sure I'm not being monitored."

"They can do that?" she said.

"You bet." RJ gave a grimace. "It's one of the pitfalls of my trade."

"But who . . ." She stopped. The answer was obvious. "Of course. The police. With all that's going on, do you really think they took the time to lay a trap?"

"Why not?" He stopped typing and glanced at her. "Look at all the effort they've put into trying to catch you. Listen. Tracking down this Juiceman is going to take a while. His information seems to be protected from outside surveillance and I don't want to stay connected too long. Let's move on."

"Can we take a look at the security tapes for three debt collectors from Las Vegas? They were after him, too."

RJ pulled up the security tapes, then wound them back until Nicole called out. "There they are! Stop!"

Three men were there, remarkably alike—thugs looking awkward in suits and ties. Each had a shaved head and self-styled facial hair. One had a colorful display of tattoos on the back of his neck that reached from below his collar onto the back of his shaved head.

"Can you get screenshots of their faces?" Nicole said.

Before RJ had a chance to do this, he glanced over at the second computer and jumped to his feet. "Oh, my God!" he shouted. "They caught me!"

He raced around the room, shutting down his computer equipment and turning off several cell phones. "The police will be here soon," he said. "I've got a record. They'll think I'm involved in the murders. I've to get out of here." His words tumbled out so fast they were almost incomprehensible.

Once everything was turned off and unplugged, he got out an overnight bag and threw some things in. He was at the front door pulling it open when he turned to Nicole. "You want a ride somewhere?"

"I'm afraid I have nowhere to go."

"Oh—in that case you can stay at my neighbor's apartment. He left town after the quake and gave me the key."

"When do you expect him back?"

"No idea," he said. "He was so freaked out he might never come back."

"So, it's okay for me to stay there?"

"Sure. Better stay away from my place, at least for tonight," he said. "The police are probably going to show up. When the coast is clear, move back here. This place is more comfortable than my neighbor's, and I've got plenty of food. You're also welcome to use my computer." He reached into a drawer in one of the worktables and pulled out several key rings. He handed them to her, his hands shaking with the urge to escape. "Here. These are to my place. These to my neighbor's. It's the only other apartment on this floor. And these are for my car. I'm taking the motorcycle."

"Thanks. I need the password for your computer."

"It's on a sticky on the side of the computer." He moved into the hall, then turned back to her. "Stay close. I'll be back in a day or two. We'll figure out another way to get at those tapes." The door slammed shut, and she heard him run down the stairs.

It wasn't long before she spotted headlights on the street. Three patrol cars were pulling up in front. With the keys in her hand, she grabbed the thumb drive, her purse, and her jacket and hurried down the hall. Dawn hadn't yet broken, and the hallway was so dark she had to feel her way along. She'd reached the neighbor's door and was fumbling with the keys when they fell out of her hand. They jangled as they hit the floor and bounced away. In a fit of panic, she dropped to her knees and felt around for them. That was when she heard the sound of feet pounding up the stairs.

CHAPTER SEVEN

NICOLE PRESSED HERSELF AGAINST THE WALL, grateful for the darkness. Down the hall, a flashlight flicked on, and she could make out the shapes of two, maybe three, forms heading her way. She crouched down and held her breath. As they grew closer, she backed farther down the hall. All at once, the figures stopped, whispered to each other, and reversed direction, heading for RJ's place.

Once she heard the door close behind them, she reached around, located the keys, and let herself into the neighbor's apartment. Inside it was stuffy and seemed even darker than in the hall. By touch, she found an overstuffed chair and sat down to wait. Sounds came from RJ's place, the scraping of furniture and echoey footsteps of the police going in and out, thumping up and down the stairs. It sounded as if they were hauling things away, most likely RJ's computers and other electronics.

As she waited, hoping they'd leave, her night without sleep caught up with her. The chair was uncomfortable, so she felt her way over to the couch, and dozed off. She woke with a start. Sun was leaking around the edges off the closed blinds. A glance at her watch told her it was 9:30 a.m. Everything was silent. She opened the door a crack and looked down the hall. There was no sign of the police. Encouraged, she tiptoed down the stairs to peek through the window in the front door. The only signs of life were two stray cats lounging on the sidewalk across the street. They scattered when she stepped out of the building. The cats, with their heightened senses, would have fled if the police were around. She was safe, at least for the moment.

She stopped by RJ's apartment on her way back. The place was torn apart. His computers and other electronic equipment were gone.

Couch cushions, bedding, towels, plus the contents of closets, dressers, and cupboards had been dumped on the floor.

Nicole knew better than to stay very long. The police might come back. She also worried they might have bugged the apartment, installed a hidden camera, or both. Even so, she allowed herself time to check out the refrigerator. It appeared undisturbed. As RJ had promised, it was packed with food, cheese, deli meats, fresh fruits and vegetables. There was even a bottle of vodka in the freezer. She paused to take in its abundance, surprised he'd been able to stash so much food away when the quake had cleared almost everything from the markets.

Since she hadn't eaten since lunch the day before, she grabbed eggs, bread, bacon, and butter and stuffed them into a grocery bag she found under the sink.

Back in the neighbor's apartment, she considered her options while she fixed breakfast. She was in a terrible situation, cut off from just about everything, including the news. This was especially upsetting when she herself was part of a developing story. She couldn't even contact a friend who might offer her a safe place to stay. But, after putting Joanna and RJ in jeopardy, she didn't want to burden anyone else.

While it was dark, she hadn't wanted to risk turning on the lights to look around the neighbor's apartment. Now that it was light, she prowled around to see what was on offer. In the tiny bedroom she found a computer sitting on a small table. It might have been useful if she'd known the password. Despite the odds against guessing the right one, she decided to give it a try. As soon as she hit the first key, the machine woke up. By some lucky stroke, it had been set up in such a way that a password wasn't required.

From his email address, she gathered that the man who lived here was Dimitri Ostrovsky. She returned to the *Los Angeles Times*'s website. Like the previous day, most of the top stories focused on the quake. The lead article quoted a geologist who predicted that another strong aftershock could sever Southern California from the aqueduct and other water sources. This would mean that seventy percent of the area's water would be cut off. The longest story focused on the earthquake's growing toll: fatalities, ER admissions, missing persons, building collapses, fires, explosions, power and telephone outages, freeway and road closures.

When Nicole scrolled down, she found her name in an updated article. It led with news of Diana's murder, which it pointed out was "the second murder in the offices of Colbert and Smith Investigations." The story said that Nicole had been spotted at the scene and that Sue Price, her lawyer, hadn't responded to the paper's request for comment. Instead, the reporter quoted a prominent criminal defense attorney, Evie Gray. The article mentioned that she had called the paper to offer her perspective on the case. Nicole had never met Evie, but had known about her for quite a while from news reports of her work in high profile cases. In the article, she said she'd be willing to meet with Nicole and discuss her options if she were to get in touch.

Nicole considered this only to dismiss it. It was possible that Gray's offer was actually a trap set by the cops. Even it if weren't, Gray would probably give her the same advice as Sue, that her only choice was to surrender. This was a non-starter. The only person she trusted to find the killer was herself. But now, dogged by the problems of investigating the case while in hiding, she'd begun to doubt she could do it.

On the other hand, she wondered how good Sue's advice might be in the current situation. Sue was a corporate lawyer who knew little about criminal defense. Maybe an experienced defense attorney would be able to offer better options.

She mulled this over while looking through Dmitri's email, Facebook page, and bookmarked websites. What interested her was how this kind of search revealed so much about the man, his life, and his priorities. Born in Ukraine, Dmitri was an active member of L.A.'s large Eastern European immigrant community. He seemed to be some kind of therapist and appeared on a website as the head of an advocacy group dedicated to helping newcomers from Eastern Europe to adjust to life in Los Angeles.

Several hours passed, and the building remained still. She decided it was probably safe to move back to RJ's. His apartment was much larger and sunnier, and she liked the idea of being close to his refrigerator. She knew the police had taken his computers, so she picked up Dimitri's machine—old and surprisingly heavy—and carried it down the hall.

By the time she resettled, she'd made a decision. Her current situation was untenable. She had to change course. Even though she suspected Evie's offer could be a trap, she decided to risk it and get in touch with her.

Earlier, before Nicole imagined she'd ever need a defense attorney, she'd read about Evie. She was known to be quiet, self-contained, and well respected by the legal community. Nicole used the web to find additional information, and Evie looked even better. She'd worked with the Innocence Project. News stories reported her success at keeping clients out of jail while awaiting trial. Several websites listed the many awards she'd received.

Although she couldn't explain why, it bothered Nicole that Evie had called the paper volunteering her views and had all but offered to represent Nicole. She was a well-established attorney, not someone who'd need to chase clients. Nicole wasn't sure what to make of it.

She wished she could call Sue and ask her opinion. But she knew that Sue was looking for a defense attorney on her behalf and doubted that she'd endorse one she hadn't picked herself. She googled Evie's contact information and called her.

"I've been thinking you might call," Evie said after Nicole introduced herself. "I'm guessing you want to be freed from the warrant. We'll have to see if that's possible. Let's get together and talk."

"Sure," Nicole said. "But it has to be somewhere I won't be recognized."

"Of course. Let's meet at Casita Mexicana in Boyle Heights. A bit of a schlepp, but it's where I see clients who need to be incognito. It's highly unlikely anyone will recognize you there. To be extra safe, wear baggy clothes and a hat or hoody of some kind. Can you meet me there at noon?"

"Absolutely. I'll see you there." As Nicole hung up, her spirits rose. She was grateful Evie was willing to see her right away. What a relief it would be to talk to someone who might be able to help.

Rummaging through RJ's closet, she located a leather jacket and a narrow-brimmed fedora, the kind worn by jazz musicians. A pair of aviator glasses completed the effect. She also found a wool scarf and wrapped it around her neck to partially cover the lower part of her face.

Checking herself in the mirror, she had to smile. In the mismatched clothes, she looked like a teenager trying to spite her parents. Her purse, a red-leather cross-body bag, looked way too conservative. She left it on the bed and slipped the burner phone into her pocket. Now she really did look different. Back on the computer, she mapped out directions to Casita Mexicana. The route was complicated because of the freeway and street closures.

RJ's car was still in front, the derelict black Volvo badly in need of a wash. The tires were bald, but it had a full tank and started up on the first try. Because she had to travel by city streets, it took over an hour to arrive at her destination.

She parked several blocks away on a street where the buildings were painted with colorful graffiti. Half the shops were out of business. As she turned the corner, she spotted a line that snaked down the block, people waiting to get into the Casita Mexicana. Chatting quietly in Spanish, they didn't seem to mind waiting.

When she reached the front door, she looked into the small white stucco building that housed the restaurant. Sure enough, Evie was seated in a back corner of a space barely big enough for its six tables. With her fair hair and stylish suit, Evie looked somewhat out of place.

The crowd in front protested when Nicole squeezed past them. She tried to explain in her half-forgotten high-school Spanish. If they understood, they didn't care that her *amiga* was inside waiting for her.

She sat down across from Evie, and the two of them exchanged small talk about the quake, where they were when it hit, and the convoluted drive to Boyle Heights. Once that was out of the way, Nicole stated her case: "The police refused to look at several likely suspects. The only person they focused on was me. I need to be able to come out of hiding so I can investigate the case and find the killer."

Evie said, "Why do you think they charged you alone without looking at other potential suspects?"

"That's the big question," Nicole said. "Maybe they felt they needed a quick solution, given the earthquake and other demands on their time. I was the one who found Jerry when he was dying. He was lying on the gun that shot him. I didn't know what it was, so I stupidly pulled it out and left my fingerprints. I was also the first to find Diana's body.

That made me an easy target. I have to say I'm surprised that homicide detectives would spend so much time chasing me when the quake has unleashed a huge crime wave."

She was interrupted when the waitress stopped at their table to take their orders. She was wearing a peasant blouse and colorful skirt, her dark hair done in two fat braids. They both asked for the daily special spelled out on a chalkboard at the front: an enchilada served with spicy pork abodabah, rice, beans, and guacamole.

When the waitress was gone, Evie said, "Tell me why you think you need to be free to investigate this case."

"Because I know I didn't kill anybody. The murderer is still at large, and the police aren't looking for other suspects. Someone has to do that, or I'm facing a trial that could put me in prison for the rest of my life. I'm a licensed investigator with a lot of experience, so I'm well-equipped to do this."

Evie took off her glasses and waggled them at Nicole. "I'm sure that's true. But there are other well-equipped investigators. I have one in my office. I need to hear why you in particular are more qualified to investigate than someone else with the same training and background. Mistrust of the police isn't enough. Many people under arrest feel that way, along with a good percentage of the population."

Nicole nodded. "Here it is. I've already done as much as I can in my current situation. I have several major leads. No one else would have found them without knowing Jerry, his problems, and his relations with people around him. I believe I'm halfway to finding the killer. But I have to be able to appear in public so I can interview people and look up police and court records. I also need access to investigative databases. To do that, I have to sign in with my name and password."

"Okay." Evie nodded. "Tell me what you've learned about Jerry so far and the people you suspect of killing him."

Nicole looked around. A couple at the next table were only a few feet away. "Here?" she said. "In public?"

Evie nodded. "I've been keeping watch on the people around us, and I'm certain no one's recognized you. They're deep in their own conversations. Just keep your voice down." She pulled a yellow legal pad from her briefcase and took notes while Nicole recounted what she knew about Jerry's gambling addiction, his debts, the Las Vegas contingent, his drinking and drug use. Next, she listed the people who had a grudge against him.

She started to describe the messages on Jerry's thumb drive but stopped when the waitress appeared with their orders. They were quiet while they ate. The food was delicious.

When their plates were almost cleared, Evie lay down her knife and fork. "You make a good argument, but I don't know if I'll be able to sell it to the D.A. If he buys it, he can recommend your release on your own recognizance, but he doesn't have the power to actually release you. His recommendation would be sent to a judge for approval. Then, if you are released, it would come with a time limit, probably a week or ten days.

"Given that you fled to avoid arrest on a murder charge," she went on, "you're in no position to bargain. In normal times, your fugitive status would disqualify you from being released on your own recognizance. But who knows? The courts and jails are in crisis because of earthquake damage, generator failures, and breakdowns in communications between the parts of the judicial system. As a result, they're freeing people who'd never be released under ordinary circumstances. By the way, you'll need to present proof you're not a flight risk. Have you spent much time abroad?"

"I've been back and forth to England quite a bit," Nicole said. "I'm sure you know how quick the UK is to respond to extradition orders. Also, full disclosure—my fiancé is a British citizen. He's in London now on business. If the D.A. or the judge think that makes me a flight risk, why can't I be put on a no-fly list and surrender my passport?"

"Oh, dear. With that UK connection, I'm sure they would consider you a flight risk. It doesn't look good." She paused and looked away. "Look, I'll communicate your request, but I certainly can't make any promises. In any case, it will take several days, maybe a week, to get an answer. I'm sorry, but I can't do anything for you until I hear back from the D.A. For the time being, you're on your own. Do you have a safe place to stay?"

"I do."

"Are you sure? Let me put it another way," Evie said. "Have you seen police anywhere near where you're staying?"

Nicole hesitated. Why was Evie asking this? If she was on her own, where she was staying wasn't Evie's concern. Finally, she said, "Yes. Night before last, they raided the apartment where I'm staying. At the time, I was hiding out in a neighboring apartment. They didn't know I was there, and they weren't even looking for me. They were after RJ, my former workmate, who was letting me stay with him.

"Before the police arrived, RJ had found a way to get into our office computer system, and we were looking at the security tapes. That's how we found the debt collectors from Las Vegas. The police had set a trap that told them RJ had broken into the system. He was alerted when they spotted him. He immediately sent me to a neighboring apartment and disappeared. The cops arrived soon after, tossed his place and took his computers. What reason would they have to come back?"

"Do not go back there." Evie paused between each word to emphasize her point. "You can never predict what the police will do. Find somewhere else to stay."

"Okay," Nicole said, although she had no intention of doing this. She wondered why Evie wasn't being more helpful. It reminded her of the experience she'd had with Sue even though the two of them were long-time friends in addition to being attorney and client. She decided this hands-off policy probably fell into the mysterious domain of legal ethics. Perhaps it was part of the same training that taught lawyers how to win just about any argument, except perhaps with another lawyer.

RJ alone had offered her a place to hide. No one else was reaching out. Considering what they had to lose, she couldn't blame them.

"Do you have a phone?" Evie said. When Nicole nodded, she went on. "Let me see it."

Nicole reached for her purse, then remembered that she'd left it at RJ's. The burner phone was in her pocket. She got it out and handed it over. After Evie took down the number, she gave it back and stood up. "I think we're done here," she said. "I'll get in touch as soon as I hear something."

Leaving the cafe, Nicole was consumed with anxiety. Evie seemed to think the D.A. would refuse her request. And, in the off chance he did grant it, he might not allow enough time for her to find the killer. Another concern was money. If she were to leave L.A. for a more secure place to hide, she'd soon exhaust her small pool of cash, and she had no way to replace it. And there was the endgame. Would anything she could possibly do put an end to this nightmare?

Chapter Eight

As Nicole walked back to her car, she looked around to be sure she wasn't being followed. As far as she could tell, no one had given her a second glance. But when she started the car and pulled onto the street, a somewhat battered beige hatchback pulled out and fell in line behind her, trailing her for several blocks. She didn't think he was following her but decided to make sure. She made right turns until she'd circled the block. He was still behind her. There was no doubt about it; he was indeed following her.

She sped up to 50 in the 35mph zone. Her tail did the same. If he was trying to be discreet, he'd failed. Could he be with the police? Weren't cops trained to know the ins and outs of covert surveillance?

Nicole had been in the same situation several times, most notably when one of the cases she was involved in went viral, and paparazzi began chasing her. She was pretty sure she had more tricks up her sleeve than whoever was behind her. Spotting a parking garage, she abruptly jerked the steering wheel and screeched into the entrance. The hatchback failed to notice and sailed by. Once inside the garage, she headed directly to the exit and went out through an alley.

She picked up her route on a parallel street and was certain she'd lost her pursuer. This made her all the more surprised when he turned up a few blocks later. This time, he followed so closely she was afraid he was going to rear-end her. She kept going faster, but he did the same.

When the road widened into two lanes, she wove between them, merging in and out of cars in the next lane. She quickly managed to put several cars between her and the hatchback. Once they reached a stop sign, she jerked the steering wheel and quickly entered the inside lane. From here, she made a sudden U-turn, heading in the opposite direction. Meanwhile, her pursuer was stuck behind several other cars back at the stop sign. After half a mile, when the hatchback was out of sight, she drove to another parallel street and reversed her direction, once more heading for RJ's.

She looked in her rearview mirror. This time she really did seem to have lost him. But when she reached RJ's street, her heart sank. The now-familiar car was parked half a block from the apartment building. As much as she wanted to drive away, she couldn't, not without first going inside and retrieving her purse. It had all her money, as well as credit cards she might have to use in an emergency.

She backed up, hoping she hadn't been spotted, and drove around the block to park on the next street. After cutting through a backyard and scaling the fence, she entered RJ's building through the rear and hurried upstairs.

By now it was late afternoon, and the place was almost dark. She was raising the window shades when she heard, "Turn around." A man was standing a few feet away, holding a gun. He was tall and thin, wearing a hoodie and a black mask that, except for eyeholes, covered his face.

"Hands in the air." He had a high voice and flat affect that made him sound like a robot. "Good afternoon." His tone was surprisingly polite, considering he had a gun pointed at her. "I'm Jerry Stephens's son. I bet you didn't know I existed."

She blinked. This had to be GuessWho from the emails on Jerry's thumb drive.

"You—" He stopped to let out a sob. "You killed him! I've been looking for him my whole life. Now, because of you, I'll never get to know my father."

"It wasn't me," she protested. "Someone else killed him." As she said this, she was comparing what he'd just said with what he'd told Jerry in his emails. He'd said he didn't want to meet him, just collect money for his purported neglect of him and his mother. This was the complete opposite. But she wasn't about to argue with a gun pointed at her. Instead, she tried another approach, staring at the gun as if hypnotized while slowly moving toward him.

"Stop or I—I'll shoot," he yelled. The hand holding the gun began to shake. Clearly, he was more frightened than she was.

Scared or not, she couldn't risk the chance that he might shoot her, or the gun might go off by accident. She shifted her eyes to the wall behind him. Despite the thumping of her heart, she tried to arrange her face in an expression of relief. "Thank God," she said to the empty space behind his right shoulder. "You're just in time!"

As she'd hoped, he couldn't resist the urge to turn and look. As soon as his attention shifted, she tried to grab the gun. He still managed to hang on, and they struggled over it. The tug of war ended with an explosive bang. It set off painful screeching in her ears, making it impossible to think. Only as the noise began to fade, did she realize that GuessWho was on the floor, and she was holding the gun that shot him.

She froze. Had she killed him? She stared at him, too horrified to squat down and check his pulse. She was tremendously relieved when he let out a moan and whimpered: "My leg—you shot me!" then shouted, "I need a doctor!"

At the same moment, she heard someone thumping up the stairs. She grabbed her purse from the table and dashed to the window. Climbing out, she made the short drop to the garage roof. She spotted a drainpipe that reached almost to the ground. Gripping it, she half slid, half climbed down. The drainpipe peeled away from the wall as she descended. When she was six feet from the ground, it broke off, dumping her into a patch of thorny shrubs. She hurt all over, but managed to get up and make it back to her car. GuessWho was now the problem of whoever had arrived. As she started the car, she realized that the person she'd heard climbing the stairs might have been RJ. But every instinct told her it would be a mistake to go back and check.

It was getting dark, and she needed a place to stop and figure out what to do next. She drove west, winding her way along city streets until she reached the flatlands of Beverly Hills. She cruised residential streets, looking for a place to park. Signs posted everywhere forbade parking except for vehicles with local-resident permits.

When a Beverly Hills police car started following her, she drove south into West L.A. and found a quiet street overhung with trees. She rolled down her window and took deep breaths until her heart stopped pounding. When she was calm again, she opened her messages on the burner to see if anyone had been trying to reach her.

At last, here was a message from Reinhardt. She opened it eagerly, hoping to hear that he'd booked a flight home or was already in L.A. She was dumbstruck when she read it.

> My darling,
>
> I've accepted a new assignment from my former employer. I know you won't be happy about it, but just hear me out. They've asked me to spend a month or so dealing with a critical issue that could mean life or death for hundreds, maybe thousands. My skills are a perfect match for this assignment, and my conscience won't allow me to walk away. Once I'm done, I'll break all connection with the agency for good. This time I really mean it. I'll return when I can. Please understand.
>
> I love you more than I can say.
>
> Reinhardt

She started to cry before she finished reading it. She'd warned him that she wasn't going to waste her child-bearing years waiting for him to leave MI6. He was the great love of her life, and now she had to make good on her threat and end their relationship. Heartbreak wasn't all she was feeling. She was also angry. She reread the message and decided his self-justification was complete bullshit and an insult to her intelligence. First was his claim that he had the perfect skill set, inferring that none of MI6's other operatives had the ability to save these people. She doubted he really believed that. Or, if he did, he was delusional. Of all of MI6's agents, surely some, if not most, shared his skillset or exceeded it.

She understood a truth she'd chosen to ignore until now. He'd never been willing to commit, nor would he ever. After he proposed and bought the ring, he postponed their wedding several times. It was already a year past the date they'd first chosen. Maybe she'd known the truth all along but had been in denial. He just couldn't give up being a spy. No promise she could extract would change that. She'd made it clear she wouldn't tolerate another defection to MI6. All she could do now was admit defeat and move on.

It was clear to her that he hadn't seen the news about Jerry's and Diana's murders or her arrest. She typed out a brief message, deliberately omitting any reference to these events. They were irrelevant to his failure to keep his promise. She wrote:

> No. I don't understand. Spare me your explanations. I warned you, and now I'm finished. I never want to hear from you again.

Unable to shake the emotions that were tearing her apart, she climbed into the back seat of the Volvo and fretted through the long night.

At 8:00 a.m. she was still awake, sitting up in the back seat of the car, staring out the window when her phone rang. The call was from Evie. "Are you sitting down?"

"Yes," Nicole whispered. She was almost afraid to hear what Evie had to say.

"The judge approved!" Evie said. "He's giving you some time on your own recognizance. I could hardly believe it. Because of the flight risk, he first insisted you wear an ankle bracelet. But get this—" She let out a giggle. "He called back to say we couldn't have one. They've released so many people that they've run out. As for surrendering your passport, they don't want it because there aren't enough people in the office to keep track of such things. So, you're on your own. He did, however, set a one-week limit on your freedom. You'd better make it count. Now you need a safe place to stay. Meet me near my office at the corner of Burton Way and LaPeer as soon as possible. We need to get you another car and a crash pad where no one can find you. Can you get here by, say, 10:00?"

"I'll be there. Does this mean I can use my credit cards?"

"Hmm, I guess so—at least for the moment. Charge away."

By the time they hung up, Nicole was smiling. She parked in the lot of a nearby McDonald's and used the bathroom to brush her teeth, comb her hair, and try to smooth out her sleep-rumpled clothes. It was hopeless, so her next stop was at a little clothing shop on Melrose that was open twenty-four hours a day. There she picked out designer jeans, an embroidered peasant top, and a jaunty fleece jacket. She paid with a credit card, harboring the childish hope that Detective Martinez would spot the purchase and track her down. Then she'd have the satisfaction of telling him the warrant for her arrest had been suspended. She was free to come and go as she pleased. He couldn't do anything about it.

She arrived at the meeting spot at the stroke of 10:00 and waited a short time before Evie emerged from an office tower carrying a large tote bag. Once Nicole was out of the car, Evie handed the bag over. It was fairly heavy, loaded with a laptop, a burner phone still in its package, a brochure for a resort, and a print-out of a map with driving directions.

Evie held up the brochure to show the cover, which featured a lagoon-shaped pool with a mini waterfall. "Here's where you'll be staying," Evie said. "The Blue Lagoon Lodge. It's in the Valley. My firm will up-front your expenses."

"That's not necessary, now that I can use my credit cards."

Evie shook her head. "Uh-uh. Remember? Using your credit cards will reveal your location to anyone tracking you. From this moment on, you're disappearing from the radar. It's important that no one knows where you are." She took a wallet out of her purse, pulled out a wad of bills, and handed it to Nicole. "Seven-hundred dollars. This should take care of you for now."

After putting the money in her purse, Nicole glanced at the brochure, then back at Evie. "This place is in Pacoima?" She could hardly believe it. Pacoima was a town of depressed neighborhoods and a hotbed of crime, noted for its robberies, home invasions, and car thefts.

"Yes." Evie gave a smile. "That's one of the reasons it makes such a good hiding place. No one would dream of looking for you there. The place is a bit funky, but it's securely gated and has everything you need. There's even a swimming pool. People we send there seem to like it. Now for your other arrangements. Would you like us to bring you anything from your home? I can have an associate go there and deliver it to you."

"I need some clothes. Three—no, four outfits, nothing dressy. I'll also need PJs and lingerie," Nicole said. "And a swimsuit and some running shoes."

"Consider it done. You'll have it late today or tomorrow morning." Evie looked Nicole over. "That's a nice outfit you're wearing. Um—do you realize you've left the price tag on your jacket?"

Nicole reached around, pulled the tag off, and stared at it. "Oh, my God," she laughed. "Did it really cost that much? I was so thrilled to be able to use my credit card, I guess I wasn't paying attention."

"You said you borrowed this car," Evie said. "These ancient Volvos are in vogue at the moment and tend to draw attention. We'll loan you something less conspicuous. My assistant will return it to the owner for you. What's the address?"

Nicole dictated RJ's address, then added, "Give me a moment to write a note explaining what happened." She found some paper in the glove compartment, dashed off a note to RJ, then folded it and handed it to Evie, along with the keys to the car and her condo.

Evie opened her purse but hesitated before dropping them in. "Tell me this note doesn't mention the Blue Lagoon Lodge."

Nicole shook her head, and Evie went on to explain the rules she expected Nicole to follow. "Tell no one where you're staying. Now that you have a new burner phone, throw away the old one. I assume you don't have your personal cell phone with you. Right?"

"Right," Nicole said.

"Good," Evie went on. "Do not give anyone the number of the new one. Do not communicate with anyone via your regular email account. I can't emphasize these things too much."

"Wait," Nicole said. "There are a couple of people I need to stay in contact with."

Evie made a face. "Listen to me! This is for your own safety. The fewer who can find you online, the safer you'll be."

"Okay. Got it." But Nicole had already decided that Joanne, RJ, and her sister Stephanie needed to be able to reach her. Joanne because she knew what was happening with the office staff. RJ because she was hoping he'd reappear and lend his computer skills to help with online searches. Stephanie, simply because she was her sister.

"The cops and the killer must be aware of what you're up to, and you don't want either of them to find you." Evie said, "So you'll need a new email address. Get one on Google or Yahoo. Send it to me and—if you must—a list of the absolute minimum number of people who need to know it. I'm talking about one or two. In this age of hackers, no information is safe. If you need to see someone, use your new email to set it up and arrange to meet them far from the Blue Lagoon. Okay, that's it. Leave the car here and follow me."

Nicole followed Evie into the building. They took the elevator to the garage, and Evie led her to a plain vanilla compact parked at the far end of the bottom level. Nicole got in and, after thanking Evie and waving goodbye, exited the garage. She drove to Beverly Glen, then over the hill into the Valley. Normally, she hated driving the freeway, but now she actually missed it. The trip took almost two hours by city streets.

The Blue Lagoon Lodge was on a sparsely populated edge of Pacoima. The landscape was barren. Unlike the L.A. basin, it was unseasonably warm. She pressed the buzzer on a locked gate in the center of a ten-foot fence. After a few minutes, a man carrying a clipboard came out, unlocked the gate, and waved her into a parking spot. He immediately relocked the gate. When she got out of the car, he handed her a key on a large key fob, which was the shape and color of the neon sign in front of the lodge.

"Welcome," he said. "I'm Peter Burnett. Ms. Gray's office let me know you're to be shown to your lodgings and aren't to be disturbed. I already have you registered." He hesitated before adding, "If you'd like, I'll show you our amenities on the way." Peter was medium height with buzzcut fair hair. He seemed pleasant enough but gave off the socially uncomfortable vibe of someone who'd spent time in a monastery or the marines. Or perhaps he was just shy.

He led her through the main building, which housed the registration desk. The interior appeared relatively unharmed by the quake except where part of a wall had collapsed and left the ceiling on a tilt. The area was blocked off by warning signs.

The social hall featured a dining room. "In ordinary times, we serve meals here, but we can't do that now," Peter said. "Part of the problem is that our staff hasn't returned since the quake. We also had some problems with the kitchen." He led her out of the building and past an outdoor pool with a rock waterfall and hot tub. A standing whiteboard announced these amenities were out of order.

"The rooms all have vibrating beds—a gift from the past. They've been so popular management has never gotten rid of them. We also have a single coin-op washer and dryer you get to share with the other guests." He winked, then blushed a bit, perhaps feeling he'd gone too far.

They exited the building. He led her to a couple of dozen small cottages painted in pastels and stopped at a lavender one. Inside, the air conditioning was going full blast, making the place uncomfortably cold. Once Peter was gone, Nicole turned it off.

Promotional brochures, like the one Evie had given her, were lying on the coffee table. She hadn't had time to read it, so she picked one up and looked it over, amused by its claims. It described Pacoima as "The Beverly Hills of the San Fernando Valley" although it bore no resemblance to that fastidiously manicured city of the rich and famous. The brochure promised a "tropical-resort-style, gated mini-estates," perhaps referring to the cottages.

She sat down at the desk and opened the laptop Evie had given her. She hadn't checked her email in days and was about to log in before remembering Evie's warning not to reveal her location online.

She downloaded a hack-proof website she'd used before. It allowed her to look at her messages and emails without being traced. Her mail was mostly junk: ads, promos, and scams, including some in Chinese. She didn't understand the latter but had heard they were demands for payment of bogus tax bills from the Chinese government. Others warned that her computer had been infected with a virus and, if she didn't call immediately, her hard drive would be erased or damaged or both. These she ignored. Messages from old friends, acquaintances, and strangers had piled up in much greater numbers. Many wanted to meet up or, at the least, find out what had happened to her. Some asked if she was okay. Others wanted "her side" of the story they'd read in the paper. These, she knew, had come from reporters or journalistic wannabes looking for a scoop.

As Nicole deleted them, she came across a name she recognized, Breanna Jones. Jones was Martinez's partner when they arrested her. She opened it and read:

> I hope you are alright. I lit a candle for you in church this morning, and I prayed for you. I know you're innocent.
>
> I have an idea. If we work together, it might help you out of your current situation. Let's meet so we can talk about it. Call me at (213) 555-9292.
>
> Please know this isn't a trap.

Nicole was certain it was exactly that, a laughably crude trap to get her to surrender to Martinez. She was shocked that Jones imagined she'd fall for it. She quickly deleted the email, along with those still left. She left her email account and turned to Google to set up a new one under a different name. This done, she sent the new address to Evie and the people she wanted to keep in touch with.

Next, she googled Garrick McVeigh, the man she'd shot in the leg who called himself *GuessWho*. The people-search website wanted $35 for a deep background check with court records. For a moment she was stumped. It was a small amount, but how could she pay when she couldn't use her credit cards? After a bit of thought, she decided to ask Peter, the lodge manager. If he put the $35 charge on his credit card, she'd offer him $50 from the cash Evie had given her. She brought the laptop with her to the lodge's office.

"Of course," Peter said. "I'll charge the $35, and you reimburse me for that amount, but please, no tip." He didn't ask why she needed to use a people search site, nor did she offer an explanation. He typed in his credit card numbers. She thanked him profusely and went back to her room to finish the job.

Sure enough, McVeigh had a rap sheet, with several arrests for minor crimes and a sentence of one year in a Kansas jail for attempted blackmail. Since then, he'd been arrested for a hare-brained, get-rich-quick scam. This led to a six-month sentence of community service. After he failed to show up, he was put in jail to serve his sentence plus a three-month penalty for failing to complete community service. Other than his arrest record, he didn't seem to exist on the internet or on social media. He had no known family, no occupation, no work record. Aside from his clashes with the law, he was an enigma.

She paused to consider what this said about McVeigh's motive for contacting Jerry. He was a convicted blackmailer and scammer. That should have explained it. But with Jerry gone, why had he followed her and held her at gunpoint while he wept about Jerry, a man he must have known wasn't his father? What had he expected to accomplish? Unless he was totally nuts, he had no reason at all. She wondered if the earlier blackmail scam had been along the same lines as his threat to Jerry. Rap sheets never revealed such details.

Still chewing on this, Nicole paused and stared out the window. On the sun-parched lawn behind the cottage, a striped, gray cat was stalking a hummingbird. It made her think of the way Martinez was stalking her.

Here was her biggest problem. Now that she was supposed to be free to investigate her case, she still had to hide from everyone so the killer wouldn't find her. But how would she be able to clear herself when she couldn't appear in public? Where would she find the information she needed or the tools essential to her search?

Just then her new burner rang. It was at the bottom of her purse, and while she was digging for it, the ringing stopped. She looked at recent calls; the last one had come from RJ. She listened to the message he'd left. "Hey, thanks a lot for leaving that weirdo bleeding all over my apartment. I mean, that was you, wasn't it? I had to call 911 and get out the way until the ambulance took him away. Where are you? I've stumbled on some pretty interesting stuff. Give me a call."

When she tapped in his number, he picked up right away. "I found out who those other messages were from. You know, the guy who calls himself Juiceman and threatened Jerry."

"Yes?" she said. "That's great! Who is it?"

"His name is Joe Martinez."

Nicole felt as if the wind had been knocked out of her. She tried to tell herself that Joe Martinez was a common name in a city like L.A. with its huge Latino population. But she knew this wasn't a coincidence.

By the time her voice returned, she understood what this meant. Homicide Detective Joe Martinez had killed Jerry and Diana. And he was bent on framing her in order to cover up his own guilt. But why had he killed Jerry in the first place? He'd arranged a huge loan for him, then threatened him for not paying it back. That didn't seem like enough motive to kill Jerry, especially after their long friendship. There had to be more to it.

Diana's murder made a certain amount of sense. She must have seen Martinez that morning, perhaps she'd even witnessed Jerry's murder. Martinez knew she'd seen him and felt impelled to get rid of her.

She found herself shivering. This new development—Martinez as both cop and killer—was terrifying. She understood that, with so much at stake, he would stop at nothing to make sure the blame rested on her.

Then another realization struck. Martinez had shown he wouldn't hesitate to kill. That meant her own life was in peril. She might not live long enough to prove her innocence or even to stand trial. She had to keep running and stay out of sight until she had irrefutable proof of his guilt.

Chapter Nine

Late that night found Nicole in her Blue Lagoon Cottage, mulling over the day's revelations. She thought about what RJ had told her and considered the threat Martinez posed. The ring of her new burner phone made her jump, startling her out of her dark thoughts. Her sister Stephanie was on the line. "Oh, Nicky! I'm so glad I found you. I've been so worried! You okay?" She was talking so fast, it was hard to understand her.

Nicole sighed, at a loss to describe her current situation. "I'm okay," she finally said. "How are you?"

"Terrible," Stephanie said. "I went crazy trying to find you. Just now I got your message with your new number."

"Are you on your own cell?"

"Of course."

"Listen. I'm hanging up now, before anyone can track this call," Nicole said. "Go out and buy a new burner phone. Use it to call me back. I'll be waiting." Without saying goodbye, she disconnected.

An hour passed. She was in bed, in a continuing state of agitation, when her phone rang again.

"Why do I need a burner phone to talk to you?" Stephanie said. "You're scaring me."

"Haven't you been reading the L.A. Times?" Nicole said.

"Yes. Sorry. I did see the story about your boss and that poor woman. That's really awful." Stephanie rushed on without giving Nicole a chance to explain what was going on. "Just listen to what happened to me. The earthquake wrecked my poor little house. It jumped off its foundation and pretty much collapsed. So I've been living out of my car—even sleeping there. It's so cold, and I've been so scared." She started to cry.

"Wait," Nicole said. "I have to know. Did you give this number to anyone else?"

"No," Steph sniffled and blew her nose. "Reinhardt called a while ago. He asked if I knew how to reach you, but I hadn't gotten your number yet. I'll give you the number he called from. After we hang up, you can call him."

Nicole sighed. "I'm not going to do that. I don't want to talk to him."

"Why not?" Stephanie said. "I thought you'd be happy to hear from him."

"I'm done with him. He went back on assignment with MI6. I warned him I'd end things if he did that again. But it's not in his DNA to turn down a chance to play spy or make a real commitment to me. For the first time, I totally get it. I can't change him, so I have to move on."

"But you love him."

"I do—did. I guess someone else might just let this slide. Figure having Reinhardt, being with him part of the time, was worth it. Of course, she'd have to accept his disappearances every few months on assignments from which he might never return. That's just not good enough for me. I want marriage and a normal family life. He's incapable of giving me that."

"I'm sorry," Steph said. "But I still don't understand. Why are you hiding out? What happened?"

"You said you saw the story in the Times."

"I did, but I barely started reading it, and my phone ran out of juice. I put it on the charger, and I guess I forgot about the story. What did it say?"

Nicole explained, as briefly as she could, what had happened, omitting what she'd just learned about Martinez. It was too frightening, and she didn't want to burden her sister.

"Oh my God!" Stephanie squeaked. "You're the most law-abiding person I know. And you're a fugitive from justice?"

"Try not to sound so gleeful about it."

"I'm not. I'm just amazed by the way you get into these situations and then, just as easily, get out of them. What's happened to you is just awful, Nick. It really is! But I'm in terrible trouble, and I really need your help."

"Like how?"

"Can I stay with you? I'm desperate. I spent a couple of nights on Tina's couch, but she kicked me out. Said I was too messy and didn't pull my weight, whatever that means. That's when I moved into my car. Please, please let me stay with you. Just until I can arrange something more permanent."

Nicole hesitated, thinking of what a terrible roommate her sister was. Still, as a big sister, she knew her duty. "Okay. But you have to be very careful that no one follows you here. You can't use your credit cards for gas or food on the way because someone could track you that way. In fact, turn off your cell and stash it somewhere safe. Just bring the burner."

"I can't. I don't have a safe place to leave it."

"Drop it in your mail slot. That should be safe. Now, I want you to promise that you won't tell anyone where I am, especially Reinhardt."

"Geeze—so many orders!" Stephanie complained. "Okay, okay."

Nicole explained how to get to the lodge and waited while Stephanie wrote it down. After they hung up, Nicole thought about her history of sharing space with her sister. As adults, each with her own place, they got on perfectly well. But when they were growing up, sharing a room, things could turn ugly. Later, on vacations and other times they'd bunked together, it hadn't gone well.

Stephanie's friend was right. She was messy in the extreme. It was as if a cloud of disorder followed her from room to room and remained after she moved on and created the next mess. Worse yet, whenever the sisters stayed together, Stephanie seemed to expect to be fed and waited on. Nicole decided to see how things went. Worst case, she could always rent another cottage, put her sister in it, and let her fend for herself.

She called Peter's office. Even though it was ten at night, he was there. She explained that her sister was going to arrive in an hour or so.

"No worries," he said. "I'll be in the office until midnight. I'll let her in."

After thanking him, Nicole got out of bed to wait. She heard Stephanie's voice before she knocked, thanking Peter for walking her to the cottage. She was almost unrecognizable in an unfamiliar down coat with a fur-lined hood that covered a good part of her face. "Can I use the facilities?" she said. "I'm dying." She hurried through the small suite, heading for the bathroom. As she came out, she looked around, wrinkling her nose as if she smelled something unpleasant. "What is this place?"

"It's my hideout. My lawyer put me here."

"Nice," Stephanie said in a tone that made it clear she didn't think it was nice at all. "Can you help me bring in my stuff?"

Nicole followed her out to her car. It was packed with clothes and small appliances from her house. After they brought in some basics, they went to bed, Nicole in the bedroom, Stephanie on the fold-out couch in the living room. The next morning, they woke up late.

"I think we should go out and find us some breakfast," Nicole said. "I didn't have dinner last night, and I'm starving."

"Well, you're in luck," Stephanie said. "I brought some things you're going to like." Out of a bag they'd brought in from her car, she produced a box of Cheerios and a container of shelf-stable milk. Lacking bowls and spoons, they improvised with the coffee mugs the lodge provided. Eating was messy because they had to use their fingers to fish out the cereal, then drink the remaining milk from the mugs.

After they were done, they spent the day playing cards and Monopoly, which Stephanie got from the trunk of her car. They talked and talked—about the quake, the misery they'd witnessed, and, as always, memories of childhood. Because of the seven-year age difference, they'd each grown up in a different house, and yet in some respects, like their parents, it had been the same. Each enjoyed telling stories about events the other had missed. Nicole, whose every thought had been focused on Martinez and the threat he posed, welcomed the diversion.

Around five they realized they were hungry again. Still chatting, they put on their jackets and headed to the office to ask Peter where they could get some food. On the way, they passed the closed dining room. At the rear, a sign on the door leading to the kitchen said, "Caution. Do Not Enter." Nicole recalled that Peter had mentioned issues with the kitchen. She wondered how much damage it had suffered.

Nicole and Stephanie stopped and looked at each other in silent understanding. They were both curious about the damage to the kitchen. Why not take a look? When they entered the dining room, they saw that the door frame leading to the kitchen had been blackened by fire. A look into the kitchen told the whole story. Fire or an explosion, probably triggered by a gas leak, had consumed the entire room. Every surface was black.

Satisfied, they went to the office and caught Peter as he was leaving. He said he didn't know of any restaurant that might be open. "Even under normal circumstances, there aren't many food places around here. In the town itself, there are some fast-food outlets, but I have no idea if any of them are open." He was silent, before adding, "There's a service station with a minimart not far from here. They've got some takeaway items, and I'm pretty sure they're open 24/7. Just turn right when you drive out of our lot. Sorry, but I'm supposed to be somewhere, and I'm late. Good luck."

After he left them, Nicole said. "I passed that gas station on the way in. It's pretty close. Why don't we walk? We can get some fresh air and something to eat."

As they walked along, they watched the sun begin to set. The clouds turned pink, then darkened to purple. When they reached the service station, they found both it and the mini-market closed. The windows had been broken and were now boarded up. They stood, looking up and down the road, from the Blue Lagoon to a pulsating red glow north of them.

"Let's turn back," Nicole said.

Stephanie was staring at the glow in the distance. "I'm so hungry my stomach hurts, and there's no food at that wretched lodge."

"Come on," Nicole said. "We'll call around and have something delivered."

"In this wasteland? You've got to be kidding. That light is telling me something's open there—a bar maybe or even a restaurant."

Stephanie started walking toward it. Nicole, who didn't want to leave her sister by herself on a deserted road, followed. After another fifteen minutes, a flashing red neon sign came into view. "Happy Hour Bar and Grill" appeared in big red letters. Below that a rotating LED message blinked out "Food! Drinks! Girls! Happy Hour 24/7!' in red, white, and blue lights. The bar itself was soon in sight, a run-down building with a wood plank façade. It looked like part of a movie set for an old western.

"Maybe it's not the kind of place we'd normally hang out," Stephanie said. "But we can get take-out and bring it back."

The women were within a few steps of the place when they sensed a vehicle behind them going at the same pace they were. They moved out of its path and watched as it rolled by, a khaki van with a sheriff's department logo on the door. Two men inside were wearing white cowboy hats, which Nicole knew weren't part of the regulation uniforms for deputy sheriffs.

"Hello, ladies," the driver said. "You're on our most wanted list. We've been looking for you."

His words made Nicole's heart freeze. She watched the van as it pulled into one of the parking spaces in front of the bar. The two men who got out were wearing tan sheriff deputies' uniforms and the white hats. Without taking their eyes off the women, they went into the bar.

When Stephanie started toward the steps, Nicole grabbed her arm. "We've got to leave!" she said. "The police are searching for me, and those deputies seem to know about it. The sheriff's office and the police don't usually cooperate, but I'm thinking these guys might have seen the all-points bulletin and are hoping to turn us in. If we run, we might be able to get back to the gas station and hide."

"Why do you always have to catastrophize?" Stephanie said. "Those guys just seemed like nerds trying to be flirty. You're the one who said it's unlikely they'd help the LAPD. And if they really are after us, there's no way we can outrun their van. I'll bet they've never heard of you. They'll harass us a bit, and we'll ignore them." Shaking off the hand Nicole put on her shoulder, she headed up the steps to the bar's front door. Once again Nicole felt she had to follow. Taking a step she'd promised herself to avoid, she felt anxiety fill her stomach, threatening to spill over.

They were greeted by a blast of warm air loaded with the smell of beer and stale cigarette smoke. The place was dim, but not enough to hide its shabbiness. Sawdust was scattered on the floor in an attempt to make it look authentic, but it was just a large, square room with no particular décor except for the mismatched wood tables and chairs. At the rear, a single bartender stood behind a door on sawhorses set up as a bar.

The deputies were standing to the right of the entrance. They stared as the women passed. "Oh, baby," one of them said, addressing his remark to Stephanie, who was tall, willowy and irresistible to men. Then he asked if she wanted a "good f—." The other's message was somewhat less offensive: "Don't worry ladies. I can protect you from this bozo." But his tone suggested this offer wasn't any better than the first.

Despite the hassle, Nicole decided Stephanie might be right. These men were acting as if they'd hoped to pick up any woman who might show up at this unlikely spot.

The menu was posted on a white chalkboard. Nicole and Stephanie paused to read it and discuss what they wanted. Meanwhile, the shouter moved forward and hovered behind them. Trying to ignore him, they walked over to the bartender. Nicole ordered the hamburgers listed on the menu.

When Nicole was done explaining what they did and didn't want on the burgers, Stephanie piped up, "Please make the fries crisp, not soggy." At last the bartender spoke up. "All I got is dogs and fries," he said. "Fries come as they are. Take it or leave it. Mustard and ketchup over there." He gave a nod to a small tray at the end of the bar with a bottle of ketchup and jar of mustard. With that, he picked up a rag and began mopping the makeshift bar.

Nicole asked for four orders of hotdogs and fries. The man kept polishing the bar as if he hadn't heard. Then, still without acknowledging their order or looking at them, he disappeared into a back room. With both deputies standing close behind them, the women grew increasingly uncomfortable. They could only hope the bartender had gone to fill their order. Nicole wondered if they should cut their losses and leave.

By the time they got their food and were back on the road, it was dark, with only thin light from the stars and crescent moon to guide them. The deputies followed them out and piled into the van.

"I don't like this at all," Nicole murmured. She was fairly sure the deputies weren't planning to drive away and leave them alone.

Yet the van remained parked as the women started toward the lodge. "Maybe we're okay," Nicole said. She was beginning to feel relieved as they put some distance between themselves and the sheriff's van. Then, all of a sudden it appeared, passing them, and turning to block their path. The van had barely stopped when the men bolted out. In an instant, they grabbed Nicole and Stephanie, cuffed their hands in front, and strongarmed them into the back of the van. The next thing the women knew, the door slammed, and the lock beeped shut.

The van started up and eventually left the road for what felt like a rocky trail that made a very bumpy ride in the back of the vehicle. Nicole hit her head; Stephanie grabbed Nicole's arm to steady herself. After a minute or two, she whispered, "What are we going to do?"

"Remember our self-defense class?" Nicole reached out with her cuffed hands and touched Stephanie's knee. She immediately understood. The main move they'd learned in their self-defense class was to knee or kick an attacker in the groin. If conditions were ideal, it wasn't that difficult. The main thing was for them to aim well and coordinate their movements. They'd only have one shot at it.

Finally, the van stopped. The back door opened, and the headlights revealed a desolate landscape at the foot of a mountain. The earth was so parched it had cracked. The men moved quickly, and there was no doubt what was on their minds. One of them grunted like a wild boar as he grabbed Nicole. He tried to pull off her blouse but only managed to rip her sleeve. Another held Stephanie in a bear hug and tried to kiss her. Nicole managed to pull back from her attacker until she had enough room to kick him mightily between the legs. He doubled up and fell to the ground moaning.

At the same time, Stephanie, who was by far the tallest, used her knee to immobilize the hugger. Before the fallen men could rally, the sisters ran to the SUV and, still cuffed, awkwardly climbed in. The engine was still running, and Nicole sped away. When they reached the gas station they'd passed earlier, she drove around back and parked the van where it couldn't be seen from the road. It took some maneuvering, but she found the key for the cuffs, both hers and Stephanie's. After they got out, Nicole threw the keys into some low growing shrubbery. They ran back to the lodge. They'd lost the hotdogs and fries somewhere between the bar and the place where the men had taken them.

They found Peter in the office. Nicole told him about the kidnapping attempt. "I know those guys," he said. "They stop by once in a while and ask if there's been any trouble. They seemed okay, even polite. My God, they must be drunk out of their minds. I'll report them to the sheriff's office in the morning."

"Thanks," Nicole said. "We brought some food back, but it got lost during our tussle with those jerks. Do you know of any place that might be open now and able to get some food to us?"

"Sorry. No. I don't have any food here. I was planning to go out tomorrow to restock. I guess you'll have to do a search on 'restaurants near me' and make some calls."

Back in their cabin, Nicole did what he suggested, using the laptop to look for restaurants within a ten-mile radius. She made a list and began calling. Nothing was open. For perhaps the first time in their lives, the sisters went to bed truly hungry.

The next morning they were up at 6:00, still hungry, but it was well before any markets would be open. Steph watched TV while Nicole went outside to sit on one of the chaise lounges surrounding the pool. She tried to get her laptop to connect with the internet without much success. The signal was weaker today. She gave up and watched some other early risers walk by, a couple with a screaming newborn and cranky toddler. As far as Nicole could tell, these were the only other guests at the lodge. It made her realize how isolated they were. She couldn't help thinking this place might not have been the best choice for a hideaway, given the danger they were in.

She heard a commotion at the front and hurried to see what was going on. To her alarm, the sheriff's van from the previous night was parked outside the high fence that surrounded the lodge complex, its front bumper resting against the gate. One of the kidnappers had gotten out of the vehicle and was arguing with Peter.

"We're here to apprehend these women. They're fugitives from the police," the deputy sheriff shouted.

"Right." Peter paused, as if considering what approach to take with the deputy. "Cool it, you guys. I can see you've been drinking. Do you want me to report you? You need to go home and sleep it off."

This made the deputy angrier. "You can't refuse to let us in. I'm a law enforcement officer. You gotta do what I say."

"If you're going to be like that," Peter said. "I'm sticking to protocol. You're drunk and a danger to my guests. You'd have to sober up and show me a search warrant before I let you in. This is private property. I have the right to turn away anyone I consider a danger. You'd better leave because I'm calling your head office. They won't be pleased to hear you've been drinking on duty and that you and your partner kidnapped my guests and assaulted them."

After he walked away, the deputies got in the van and backed up. But, instead of driving away, the vehicle crashed into the gate, smashing it. The deputies got out and stepped onto the lodge's grounds.

They'd advanced only a few feet before Peter was back, waving a handgun. He raised it in the air and shot twice. The men retreated into their vehicle and drove onto the road. The van seemed damaged from crashing through the gate. The tires made a clunking noise as they drove away.

Nicole came out from the shadows where she'd been hiding. "Thanks, Peter. I hope those guys leave us alone, but they seem pretty determined."

"As I said, I know them," he said. "Their behavior is completely out of control. They must have been drinking all night. We can only hope they go home and sleep it off. If they were to come back—and I don't think they will—I'm calling the sheriff's head office. You're safe here."

Nicole didn't find this reassuring. As she headed for their room, she understood they couldn't stay at the Blue Lagoon any longer. They had to move. She decided to call Evie, her defense attorney, so she could ask her to find another place for them to hide. She stopped outside the cottage and called the cell phone number Evie had given her. The phone rang and rang, but there appeared to be no way to leave a message. Next, she tried the law firm and was surprised to get a recorded message saying the office was closed until Monday. Only then did she realize it was Friday. She checked her watch. It was a few minutes past 5:00. Of course they were closed, although it did seem strange they didn't give another number for emergencies. Except for Peter, she and Stephanie were on their own for the next two days.

CHAPTER TEN

As soon as she got up, Nicole pulled on jeans and a sweater. She went on to choose her outerwear, hoping to disguise her appearance from her limited wardrobe. Instead of her coat, she picked an oversized quilted jacket and a dark printed scarf to cover her blonde hair. Checking in the mirror, she was pretty sure no one would recognize her, except perhaps Martinez. But it wasn't likely he'd be cruising the streets in Pacoima looking for her.

Although it was only 6:45, Peter was already in the lodge's office. "We're both starving," Nicole said. "We're going out to scare up something to eat. Can you recommend somewhere that might be open?"

He nodded. "I don't think local restaurants will be open for a while, but Foothill Ranch Market is a good bet. They have packaged sandwiches and the like. It's on Pacoima's main road." After he explained how to get there, Nicole hurried back to their room to wake up Stephanie and insist she come along. Her presence would serve as part of Nicole's disguise. No one would expect her to be with a companion. Besides, Stephanie's height and figure drew all the attention when the two appeared in public.

The street where they parked gave them a look at what the quake had done to the small town. It seemed as if every third building had been flattened, burned down, or suffered some kind of structural damage.

Predictably, the shelves of the market were mostly empty. Nicole found ketchup, beer and pretzels, but not much else. The clerk and only employee was a woman with a frizzy ponytail. She had prominent front teeth and talked with a lisp. "We pretty much got nothin' left," she said as they checked out. "Why don't you go down the road to the food bank? I heard they got restocked this morning. People say the county's going to airdrop water, food, and other stuff this afternoon. I can't wait!"

Nicole and Stephanie walked along shops with boarded-up windows until they reached a pop-up food bank in the middle of the town square. A lot of locals were there, waiting to pick up supplies. Most were friendly, in the collective good mood that sometimes accompanies the days following a community disaster. When Nicole and Stephanie reached the head of the line, they were each handed a turkey sandwich and a cup of coffee. They stepped aside and hungrily devoured the food before moving on to the next table. There, a woman in a gingham apron gave them each a bag containing bread, crackers, peanut butter, jam, and orange soda. It didn't offer a lot of variety but was enough to see them through a day, maybe two.

When they got back to the car, a sheriff's van was parked behind them. Nicole did her best to appear calm, but she was shaking as she got in the car. She started up and cautiously pulled into the street.

Stephanie turned to look out the rear window. "That sheriff's van is following you!"

"It's not the guys from last night, is it?" Nicole said.

"I can't really see his face. But it's just one guy, so maybe it's not."

"Okay. Stop looking at him. I'm going to keep driving as if there's nothing's wrong, and I couldn't care less that he's tailgating me."

At that moment, the cruiser turned on its siren and flashing red light. Nicole pulled over and turned to Stephanie. "Let me handle this. Okay?"

Nicole rolled down the window and was slightly reassured when she saw that Stephanie was right. She'd never seen this deputy before. He had a buzzcut, a square jaw, and aviator shades. It was impossible to read his expression.

"One of your taillights is out," he said. "Can I see your car registration and driver's license?"

Nicole swallowed hard. She couldn't let him see her driver's license because it had her name on it. "Sorry," she said. "I left it home."

"Your registration?"

She opened the glove compartment, located a registration card, and handed it over. Since this was a loaner car she'd gotten from Evie, she had no idea who it was registered to. "This isn't my car," she explained. "I borrowed it from a friend. I can give you her phone number, if you like."

The deputy ignored this and stepped behind the car. Nicole knew he was checking the license plate to see if the car had been reported stolen. When he returned, he was holding his ticket book.

"I'm afraid I'll have to give you a citation because you failed to have your driver's license with you. You'll have to pay a fine and present your license at the DMV to clear the ticket. Your name?"

Nicole was prepared. "Stephanie Barnes. My address is—" She couldn't recall her sister's address, so she made one up. "860 Elm Grove Avenue, North Hollywood."

"Nickie," Stephanie murmured reprovingly.

Nicole ignored her. She was thinking how absurd it was for a deputy sheriff to be handing out traffic tickets in the aftermath of a quake that had all but flattened the city. Meanwhile, the deputy jotted the information on the ticket and handed it to her. She waited until his car turned the corner and disappeared before starting back to the lodge.

"Thanks a bunch for getting me a traffic ticket with the wrong address," Stephanie said. "How am I going to straighten that out?"

"Sorry, but I couldn't very well give him my name, could I?"

"I guess not. But really, Nicole."

They drove the rest of the way and walked back to their room in silence. Stephanie turned on the TV.

Regular programming seemed to have been reinstated. She got out her yoga mat so she could exercise while watching a rerun of Jeopardy. Nicole plopped down on the couch and tried to decompress. When her phone rang, she hurried into the bedroom and closed the door.

It was RJ, finally calling back. "Listen," he said. "I found some stealth software that will let you into the office's computers and surveillance tapes without detection."

"What is it?"

"It's malware I found on the dark web called Lockbit."

"Malware?" she said. "Isn't that something we're supposed to avoid?"

"Only if someone's using it to sneak into your computer and shut you down. Hackers use it to steal content and blackmail people. You know, 'Pay up or we're going to wreck your hard drive or release your confidential data to the public.'

"But in this case, malware is working for you," he went on. "I've used it to get into a firm's computers and see what's there. Here's the bottom line: I found another email exchange between Juiceman and Jerry with Juiceman making some pretty heavy threats. Let's meet so we can go over this stuff together. You know, two heads, better than one."

"Not here." Nicole said. "I can't tell anyone where I am—not even you. Let me figure out a safe place for us to meet. I'll call you back. Okay?"

"Of course."

After they hung up, Nicole paced the room, debating whether to meet RJ or play it safe and stay put. Unable to decide, she went outside and walked along a path that wound between the bungalows. It took her a while, but she decided that RJ was offering a way to find useful information, and information was exactly what she needed.

Back in the cottage, Stephanie was lying on her yoga mat watching TV. Nicole returned to the bedroom and used the computer to search for a restaurant where she was unlikely to run into anyone she knew or who knew her. After locating some, she started calling to see if they'd be open for lunch. Several didn't answer. One had a voice message explaining they were closed until further notice. Finally, someone at a place called *Best Burger in the World* in Thousand Oaks picked up. A woman with a thick Southern accent said, "Good morning. This is Best Burger." When asked about lunch, the woman drawled, "Yes, ma'am, we're here all day and evening. Y'all welcome to come by any time."

Nicole called RJ back and they agreed to meet there at noon. This done, she left the bedroom and turned off the TV to get Stephanie's attention. "What the hell," Stephanie said.

"I have to go somewhere," Nicole said. "I need to borrow your car. I'm afraid to use the one I came in after that deputy stopped us."

"No. You can't—"

Nicole's nerves were on edge. "I really need it, Steph!" she said. "I can't risk being stopped like that again."

"I know you're stressed," Stephanie said, "but you didn't let me finish. My car is out of gas. That's why you can't borrow it."

"Sorry. Didn't mean to snap. Okay, okay—I've got an idea. I'll be right back."

Peter was in the office, staring out the window.

"I need to drive to the far Valley," she said. "I'm afraid to take my own car. When we went into town, we were stopped by another deputy sheriff. Can you get me a rental? I don't have a credit card, but I do have some cash." She reached into her purse for the money Evie had given her.

"Not today, I'm afraid," he said. "The only car agency in Pacoima closed when the earthquake struck. Why don't you take my car? It's the gray Chevy parked 'round back. I'll use my bike if I need to go anywhere."

"One more thing," she said. "I'm worried about our safety. Can you move us to the very back of the property? Two separate cottages this time, not adjacent."

"No problem," he said. "Your lawyer left credit card information to take care of anything you might need."

He handed over his car keys. Nicole went back to the cottage to grab her laptop and jacket. She invited Stephanie to come, but she opted to stay put.

"You're going to miss out on some fine food," Nicole warned.

"I'll take my chances," Stephanie said. "Take pictures of your lunch and send them so I can feel good about my PBJ sandwich."

The drive to Thousand Oaks without the freeway was long and tedious. She couldn't help thinking of Martinez, his existential threat, and the risk she was taking by meeting RJ. Eventually, her thoughts drifted to Reinhardt. The ache of missing him made her wonder if she'd made a mistake breaking up with him. Before long, these musings were replaced by her growing discomfort as the car began to heat up. It was February, and the weather in the L.A. basin was moderate, the temperature sometimes rising to 70. The Valley was always warmer, and today even more so. According to the temperature gauge on the dashboard, it was almost 80. She tried several times to turn on the air conditioner, but it didn't seem to work.

When a fallen stretch of the 101 came into view, she couldn't resist pulling over to take a look. The quake had broken the freeway's supports, and a section had fallen, leaving a wide gap in the normally busy road. Today there was no traffic. Nor was there any sign of the cars that must have fallen off and crashed to the ground when the quake struck.

She got to the restaurant first. RJ was nowhere in sight. She went inside and bought a soft drink from the cashier, a blowsy, middle-aged blonde. "You the lady who called?" she drawled. "The place is yours. Take any table y'all want."

Nicole looked around. Except for her and the cashier, the place was empty. Even so, she picked a table off to one corner where she and RJ would be able to have a private conversation even if other people showed up. While she was waiting, she decided to make use of the time to download the app RJ had told her about. She pulled her laptop out of its case, hoping she'd be able to break into the firm's computer system, too. But getting onto the dark web and finding the app was much trickier than she'd imagined.

When she next checked the time, thirty minutes had passed and there was still no sign of RJ. She began to worry. When she tried to call him, his phone went directly to voicemail. Even more frustrating, she couldn't leave a message because his mailbox was full.

After several more unsuccessful attempts, she gave up. He wasn't coming. In the past, he'd been both reliable and punctual. She had the feeling something had happened to him, something bad. On the drive back to the lodge, she went over the possibilities. Had Martinez figured out their connection and taken him in or done something worse to him? Of course, his disappearance might have nothing to do with her, a sudden illness, an accident on his motorbike. It could be anything.

She ran into heavy traffic on the main road that carried people across the San Fernando Valley. It was late afternoon by the time she reached the lodge, daylight already beginning to dim. She went directly to the office to return Peter's keys. He wasn't there, and the door was locked. She shoved the keys through the mail slot and hurried to her cottage.

Stephanie had used chewing gum to attach a note to the front door: "Peter moved us to the back. Now I have my own cottage. Ha ha. Come to number 24, and I'll give you the key to yours."

Nicole followed Stephanie's directions to number 24 and was surprised to hear two voices, Stephanie's and Peter's. She knocked on the door. There was a long pause and some laughter before Stephanie opened it. Behind her, Peter got up from the couch and tucked in his shirt before coming to the door.

"I guess I should be going," he said.

"Thanks for lending me your car," Nicole said. "I dropped the keys in your mail slot." Just then she spotted a cell phone on the coffee table. "Wait!" she said, picking it up and offering it to him. "You forgot your phone."

He gave it a cursory glance and patted the pocket of his shirt. "Thanks, but mine's right here. I think that belongs to your sister."

He left as Nicole turned to Stephanie. "Don't tell me this is your phone!" When her sister's face turned pink, she added, "Why would you bring it with you when I told you not to."

"I didn't think it was that big a deal," Stephanie said. "Besides, I've kept it turned off except when I check messages. I haven't made any calls or sent anything out. How could anyone track me?"

Nicole tried to stay calm. It didn't do any good getting mad. Even as a child, Stephanie refused to follow rules, invariably protesting that she hadn't understood. She knew that arguing would get her nowhere, but she couldn't resist correcting Stephanie's idea that it wasn't a big deal. "They can track you even when your cell is turned off. Maybe we got lucky, and no one thought to check on you as a way of finding me. But we can't take that chance. We have to get away from here—like now."

"Sorry, Nick. I really didn't know." This time she sounded truly contrite.

Nicole picked up the phone, pulled out the sim card, and flushed it down the toilet, even though she figured it was probably too late. "Where are my clothes and what's left of our stuff from the food bank?"

"Our clothes are there." Stephanie pointed to a corner of the room, where a pile of clothes was on the floor. "I ate the rest of the food. There wasn't much."

"Okay," Nicole said. "Pack up your things. Mine, too. Here's the key to my cottage. I'm going to see if Peter can get us another place to stay."

She caught up with Peter as he was settling back in his office. "Stephanie brought her cell along," she said, "It's possible she was tracked. That means we have to move. Do you think we can use the attorney's credit card for this?"

"Sure," he said. "They told me to use it for anything you need. Sorry to see the two of you go, but if you need to stay somewhere else, I'll arrange it."

Nicole waited while he made the calls on speaker. He first reached motels with voice messages saying they were closed, probably because of the earthquake. Finally, at an Economy Inn in Tarzana, he was able to book them. After hanging up, he said, "They just had a single room. I know you prefer not to share, but we don't have much choice. It's a plain roadside motel, but Yelp says it's clean and comfortable, although it got a low rating for service. But it has the essentials: air conditioning, microwave and fridge. If you don't like it, let me know, and we'll try to find someplace else."

"One more thing," Nicole said. "We need to take Stephanie's car, but it's out of gas. Any suggestions?"

"I keep a couple of gallons in the storeroom for emergencies," he said. "That should get you to a gas station. If the one down the road is closed, you can go into town and fill up there." He paused and gave her a searching look. "I don't know what you're running from, but it sounds pretty serious. I can lend you a gun if you're comfortable using one."

"I am. I really would feel safer if I had a weapon to protect us. And thanks for not asking how we got into this predicament."

Peter went to a cabinet, got out some keys, and unlocked one of his desk drawers. He pulled out a small handgun and handed it to Nicole along with a container of bullets. "It's not loaded," he said.

He went to the storeroom to retrieve the gas and met the sisters by Stephanie's ancient Volkswagen. As they waited for him to empty the fuel into the gas tank, Nicole remembered the problem with her sister's phone. "Look, Steph," she said. "Why don't you leave your cell with Peter?"

Steph pulled out the phone and looked at it longingly before handing it over. "I was expecting some messages. But I guess that'll have to wait." She looked at Peter and added, "I'll be back for it."

Peter smiled at her. "I look forward to it." Stephanie smiled back, and they gazed into each other's eyes.

"Look, kids," Nicole said. "I hate to break this up, but we really need to go."

Stephanie started to get into the driver's seat, then changed her mind and handed the keys to Nicole. "Why don't you drive? You're the one with a sense of direction."

Nicole used her phone to get directions to the motel. After stopping in town to fill the gas tank, she drove to Tarzana. Both were quiet. Nicole was focused on two worries: whether they were safe from Martinez, at least for the moment, and what could have happened to RJ.

When they pulled into the Economy Inn, there were only a few cars in the parking lot. This made Nicole wonder if they might have more empty rooms than they'd indicated on the phone. The structure was low slung, nondescript, and utilitarian, reminding her of the modest motels where their family had stayed when she was a child.

Nicole went into reception. The check-in desk was unattended. She rang the bell. After several minutes a matronly woman emerged from a closed door behind the desk. She seemed annoyed at the interruption.

"There are two of us. I'm wondering—" Nicole began.

"I have a single room." the woman snapped. "We're full up. I explained that on the phone." She slapped the key down on the counter along with a map showing the location of their room. Then she disappeared through the door. There was a clicking sound when she locked it.

Their room, which turned out to be on the second floor, was clean, although small enough to be cramped with the two of them. It was all beige except for a shiny maroon bedspread with three neon yellow throw pillows.

Once they'd moved in, Nicole left Stephanie watching TV, and took her laptop down to the motel's empty reception room. Settling into a corner, she went to work on her computer trying to get started with Lockbit, the application RJ had recommended. This time she was able to install it. Once she figured out how it worked, she was connected to the firm's computers and started looking at Jerry's emails predating the ones on the thumb drive. Here she found more messages between him and Juiceman/Martinez ranging over several years, two or three a month. In the beginning, these were mostly lunch plans, although sometimes they arranged to meet up for ballgames. They seemed to have a solid friendship. Then, in the last six or seven months, they'd fallen out. It seemed to stem from the loan Martinez had arranged for Jerry to cover his gambling debts.

The detective didn't seem to mind setting up the initial loan of $250,000. None of his messages mentioned the source. But, with its forty percent interest rate, it clearly wasn't from a bank or credit union. A few months later, Martinez started chiding Jerry for missing several loan payments while continuing to gamble and lose money. At this point, Jerry asked Martinez to set up a second loan, this time for $150,000. This time he was turned down. Nicole found it hard to understand why Jerry thought he could get a second loan when he'd failed to keep up with payments on his first. The only reason she could imagine was that Jerry had some kind of hold over Martinez. Perhaps he'd threatened to tell the LAPD that one of their detectives was affiliated with loan sharking, which was illegal.

Martinez's warnings became more frequent and more adamant. Jerry, he said, would face serious consequences if he didn't make up the missed payments and start paying on time. Jerry offered his wife, Melanie, as collateral. Presumably he was joking.

This made Martinez angry. "You'd better start making payments, or you'll face serious consequences," he warned. "Think of the worst thing that could happen to anyone and imagine someone doing it to your family. Maybe you don't care about your wife, but what about those little kids you dote on? Because something terrible is going to happen to you and your family if you don't get with the program. These aren't the kind of people you want to mess with."

The threat chilled Nicole. Jerry's reply to Martinez sounded as if he hadn't taken the threat seriously, although he'd confessed to her that he was afraid. "You can't scare me no matter how hard you try," he'd written. "Bring them on."

There were several more messages from Juiceman. Before she had a chance to read them, the screen on her computer dimmed. The emails disappeared to be replaced by an image of a shadowy figure holding a magnifying glass. In large type at the bottom of the screen it said, "Warning! You have been seen. Sign out immediately." She scrambled to shut down the computer.

All she could figure out was that RJ had been wrong when he said Lockbit was foolproof. It hadn't hidden her presence on the firm's computers after all. It made her think of RJ and his disappearance. Had someone caught him hacking into the system? Was that the reason he was missing?

And who was doing the tracking? That was the scariest part. Was it Martinez? Had he found her location? Did this mean she had to find yet another place to hide? Or were these attempts futile, and there was nothing she could do to prevent the detective from closing in on her?

Chapter Eleven

Leaving the motel's reception room, Nicole noticed that the check-in desk was unattended, the door behind it closed. She began to feel uneasy as she walked into the parking lot. It was empty except for Stephanie's car, which they'd arrived in. The half dozen cars that were parked there earlier were gone. Deserted, the place seemed vaguely threatening.

As she rounded the corner and headed for their room, she heard screaming—no words, just shrill, high shrieks. Certain it was Stephanie, she sprinted up the stairs leading to their room. At the top she saw a stranger half lifting, half dragging Stephanie out of their room. She was screaming, kicking, and beating at him with her fists.

It wasn't Martinez. This man was tall and muscular, dressed in ratty jeans and a utility jacket covered with pockets. His black stocking cap was pulled down, covering his forehead and ears. When she was a few yards away, she reached into her bag and got out the gun Peter had lent her, letting it dangle by her side.

"Let go of her," she shouted.

Instead of answering, he pulled some plastic handcuffs out of his pocket and used them to attach Stephanie to the railing. He turned toward Nicole and opened his mouth as if to say something, then closed it when he saw she was pointing a gun at him.

"Raise your hands," she said. Then, when he complied, "Lean against the wall with your hands on it."

Instead of doing this, he ducked behind Stephanie, who was bent over, struggling to free herself from the handcuffs. He grabbed her hair and yanked, pulling her upright. She screamed again. He whipped out a gun and held it to her head. With his mouth to her ear, he shouted,

"Shut the fuck up!" By now, Stephanie was crying so hard she would have collapsed if the man hadn't been holding onto her hair.

"I'll shoot her if you don't do exactly what I say," he said to Nicole. "Toss your gun on the ground, put your arms up, and walk toward me."

Nicole let the gun drop and moved toward him. Now she could see how weathered his face was. He appeared to be much older than Martinez. When she was close enough, he let go of Stephanie, grabbed Nicole, and handcuffed her hands in front of her. He jerked her around to face the stairway.

"We're going down those steps real nice and easy-like," he said. "You lead. If you try to escape or pull some kind of trick, I'll shoot you and your buddy back there. And don't bother screaming. You can see how much good it did her."

Nicole was relieved that he was leaving her sister behind. She wondered how long it would be before someone happened along and released her. It might take hours, but eventually the police would be called. Stephanie was safe.

Now she had to figure out how to escape her kidnapper. At the moment, he was in control, pressing the gun between her shoulders as they went down the stairs. At some point he'd let down his guard. She'd have to be ready. As they headed toward the rear of the motel, she could still hear her sister yelling for help.

When they reached a maroon sedan parked next to the fence, the man forced Nicole into the rear seat. Relieved that he hadn't put her in the trunk, she sized up the situation and knew what she had to do. She waited until the car gathered speed before she got up and stood behind the driver's seat.

"What are you doing? Sit the fuck down!" he yelled, taking his hands off the wheel and trying to push her back onto the seat. With no one steering, the car veered toward the road's center line. He grabbed the wheel just in time to avoid a head-on collision with a car going in the opposite direction.

The sudden jerk made Nicole lose her balance, and she fell back onto the seat. When she got up, she could see his eyes in the rearview mirror. Instead of watching the road, he was looking at her.

"Sit down!" he screamed. He awkwardly tried to shove her away while keeping one hand on the steering wheel and looking back and forth between her and the road. This was the moment she'd been waiting for. She pulled her cuffed hands over his head and slid them down until the plastic bands were pressed against his throat. Then she leaned back and pulled as hard as she could.

The man let go of the wheel, grabbing at her hands and trying to push them away. This put tremendous pressure on Nicole's hands and wrists. Despite the pain, she kept pulling. Even if she'd wanted to release him, she couldn't. Her hands were anchored in place by the cuffs.

The man started screaming, then choked, and grew more frantic in his effort to free himself. Fortunately, traffic was light. The few approaching cars were pulling over to get out of the way.

At last he went limp, but not before the car was completely out of control. His foot must have been pressed to the accelerator. If anything, the car sped up a bit, zigzagging along the highway. After a struggle, she was able to pull her hands up and over his head. She grabbed the wheel and turned it sharply to stop the car from crossing to the wrong side of the wide boulevard. The sharp turn made the car careen off the road and crash into a tree. This brought it to a stop. The impact threw Nicole onto the rear seat again.

Unhurt, she climbed out and got into the front seat. The man was completely still. His swollen, red face was a horror—his mouth gaping, eyes protruding, the whites the color of blood. There were scratches down his cheeks, and his lips were swollen, tongue protruding. A trickle of blood leaked out of one ear. She tried to find a pulse and, failing to find one, knew that he was dead. This left her feeling both relieved and upset. She knew the choice had been her life or his. Still, killing another person, even in self-defense, was a terrible thing.

She struggled against the handcuffs, but this only seemed to make them tighter. The glove compartment contained nothing to cut through them. She undid the man's seat belt and started searching through the many pockets in his jacket. The first thing she found was his wallet. Sure enough, it held an LAPD ID card identifying him as Ronald Blithe, a detective with Robbery-Homicide who had to be a colleague of Martinez. She had no doubt that he was the one who'd enlisted Blithe to kidnap her and—she was fairly certain—kill her. She wondered what kind of power Martinez had over Blithe to force him to commit such a crime. In another pocket, she found a Swiss Army knife. With a little effort, she cut through the cuffs. Underneath, her wrists were red and badly chafed.

She cut off a section of the man's sleeve and used it to wipe down any prints she might have left on the car's surfaces. This done, she got out of the car and walked away. Several cars passed, but no one slowed or seemed to notice her as she headed back to the motel. To remain inconspicuous, she followed a path hidden from the road by oleander bushes and orange trees. It was about a mile to the motel, a walk she wouldn't have found difficult under normal circumstances. Today it took enormous effort to keep going.

When she arrived, she heard Stephanie still calling for help. She hurried up the stairs and found her still tethered to the rail. She stopped yelling as soon as she saw Nicole. "My God!" Her voice was hoarse from shouting. "I thought he was going to kill you. How did you get away?"

Nicole bought some time before answering, bending down to scoop up the gun she'd tossed earlier. She thought of the dead man's face, his grimace and protruding eyes. Unable to bear talking about it, she shook her head. "I'll tell you later." She dropped the gun into her purse and used the knife to cut off Stephanie's cuffs. Her wrists were even more raw than Nicole's. They went back in the room to run cold water over them.

"But what happened to that man?" Stephanie insisted. "How did you get away?"

"Don't worry," Nicole said. "He won't bother us again."

"But who was he?" Stephanie insisted. "Why did he attack us?"

At this point, Nicole understood that Stephanie wouldn't stop asking until she got an answer. "I'm pretty sure Detective Martinez had him come after me," she said.

"But how—"

"Please, Steph. We need to focus. We're going to grab our stuff and get out of here. Now, this minute!"

Nicole, too, was wondering how Martinez or Blithe had found them. She had Stephanie sit in the car while she looked for a tracking device.

She found nothing in the car itself, but when she searched her coat, she found a tiny one in her left pocket. It was much smaller than the one RJ had dropped in her purse, and she had no idea how it had gotten there. She tossed it to the ground.

As they drove away, Nicole tried to think of a place for them to spend the night. After their experience hopscotching motels, she decided to cross that off her list. Their only choice was to find a street where they could park and spend the night. She drove up to Mulholland at the crest of the Santa Monica Mountains that divided the city from the San Fernando Valley. After following it a while, she turned right on Laurel Canyon Blvd and drove back down into the L.A. basin. When she found a quiet spot on a steep, dead-end street, she parked.

Stephanie, who'd been sleeping for most of the drive, sat up. "Why are we stopping here?"

"We can't stay at another motel. So we have to sleep in the car. It's pretty cold, but we can use some of the clothes we brought along to keep warm. I'll get them out of the trunk. We just have to do this tonight. Tomorrow my lawyer will be back in her office, and she'll find us somewhere to stay. You're taller than me, so you get the back seat."

Stephanie got out of the passenger seat and into the back. "Can we talk about what happened with that guy?" she said.

"Sorry. I'm too worn out."

"I'm tired, too." Stephanie curled up on the back seat. "Goodnight."

"Night." Nicole climbed over the gear shift to the passenger side, hoping to sprawl out without the constraint of the steering wheel. But with the center console pressing against her back, it was too uncomfortable to lie down. She sat up and moved the seatback down. But, after another traumatic day, she was too wired to sleep, and the man's death weighed on her. No matter what he'd been up to, she felt responsible. She thought about what would have happened if she'd surrendered to the police in the first place. There would have been no attempted kidnapping, no ordeal for Stephanie, and Ronald Blithe, homicide detective, would still be alive. She stared at the dark city below and wondered how she'd ended up in so much trouble.

She woke with a start in broad daylight and checked her watch. To her surprise, it was 9:30 a.m. Although she felt as if she hadn't slept, she must have eventually dropped off. She checked on Stephanie, who was still sleeping, before getting out of the car and dialing the law firm's number. A receptionist picked up and put the call through to Evie.

They hadn't spoken since Nicole learned that Martinez had killed Jerry and Diana. She described everything that had happened since then, including her discovery that the would-be kidnapper was Martinez's colleague in Robbery-Homicide. She didn't mention how she'd managed to escape.

"Martinez not only killed Jerry and Diana," Nicole said, "he's been trying to get rid of me. He picks up our trail no matter what we do or where we go."

"I don't understand," Evie said. "Did he or anyone else mention his alleged connection with those murders?"

"No. I figured it out myself."

"What proof do you have?" Evie said. "How are you going to prove it to the D.A. or to the court? Did you actually see him follow you? And what about the man you say tried to kidnap you? How can you be sure he was conspiring with Martinez?"

"You're right," Nicole said. "I need to find out more. But I still have enough time to do that."

"Not much—just two days. And what's your plan if you can't find adequate proof by then?"

"You said you could ask the district attorney for an extension."

"I can," Evie said, "but I seriously doubt he'll grant it. And I have to tell you something else. Martinez called me first thing this morning. He wants me to persuade you to surrender."

"To him?"

"That's right. He said it would go easier on you than if you waited for the LAPD to catch up with you. There's some truth to that. Of course, I pointed out that you still have two more days. He wanted to know what will happen when that time is up, and the police put out another all points-bulletin. I want to know, too. Are you willing to keep running when you have little chance of escape? Frankly, I was assuming that you'd want to surrender at that point. It's what I strongly recommend."

Nicole didn't like the way this was going. Evie wasn't listening. Or, if she was, she didn't believe her. The same loss of faith went the other way. Nicole wasn't sure Evie would act in her best interest. "If I were to surrender, would you have your office investigate Martinez?"

"Of course," Evie said. "We'll leave no stone unturned. I'll do everything I can for you. We'll determine what's in your best interest. Maybe we can arrange a plea deal rather than letting you go to trial. Now, I have somewhere for you to stay for a couple of days. There's a fitness center near my office. Bring your sister and meet me in front of it. I'll pick you up and take you to your new lodgings."

Nicole agreed, even though she had no intention of meeting her. By the time they were done talking, Stephanie had woken up and moved to the passenger seat. Nicole started the car. Still without a clear idea of where she was going, she turned around and headed over the hill and into the valley.

"Um," Stephanie said. "Where are you going? I thought we were meeting with your lawyer, and she was going to find a new place for us to stay. Isn't her office in Beverly Hills?"

"I changed my mind," Nicole said. "We spoke, and all she could talk about was having me surrender—to Martinez, if you can believe it. She also mentioned a plea deal, which would have me pleading guilty, forgoing a trial, and serving a prison sentence for something I didn't do. I don't trust her, and she certainly doesn't trust me. I'm going to drive out of town a bit. We'll find a coffee shop, stop for breakfast, and figure out where we go from here."

CHAPTER TWELVE

AFTER DRIVING TO THE FARTHEST REACHES of the Valley, Nicole and Stephanie came to their destination—one of the Hollys coffee shops that dotted roads all the way to Northern California. At 11:00 a.m., it was fairly empty.

As soon as they sat down, a waitress served them coffee and handed them menus. Once they were alone again, Stephanie said, "Hey! I thought of somewhere no one would dream of looking for you. Do you remember that place in the mountains where we used to stay when we were kids?"

"I'm not sure. There were several."

"This was a cabin near Lake Tahoe. Dad borrowed it from a friend— Ed somebody. Can't remember his last name. I think he owned the neighborhood drugstore. The cabin was in a place called Twin Pines. The cabin was knotty pine, inside and out, and smelled of fir trees. Outside there were giant ants."

"Oh," Nicole said. "I remember those ants. It really hurt when they bit."

"Those are the ones. Not sure if the cabin is still there. We had nothing to do, no TV, no books, nothing, so we used to snoop around the vacant cabins. Sometimes we managed to break in. We'd explore and, like, steal food."

"Weren't we adventurous?" Nicole wondered where this story was going.

"My point," Stephanie said, "is that, at least back then, those cabins had almost no security. If we went there, we could find one, and we'd be safe. You know how to pick locks, so getting in wouldn't be a problem.

You could keep doing research on your computer. It would give you time to find what you're after."

"That's quite a drive," Nicole said. "Even under normal circumstances, it's seven or eight hours. After the quake, with the roads messed up and a lot of freeways closed, it could take twice that long, if we could actually get there."

"That's the worst case," Stephanie said. "We don't know if the damage extends that far from L.A."

"We don't know that it doesn't."

"Well, if that's too far, how about—"

The ringing of Nicole's burner interrupted them. It was the one Evie had given her. She'd been intending to throw it away and get a new one. But she hadn't had a chance. She pulled it out of her purse and stood up, intending to throw it in the trash. But she couldn't resist glancing at caller ID. It said R. Reinhardt. She was so surprised that she hit answer, even though she'd vowed to never speak to him again.

"I'm back," Reinhardt said. "I headed home as soon as I found out you were in trouble. If you were trying to drop off the grid, you've succeeded. Where are you?"

"How did you get this number?" she said.

"I have my ways. Are you going to tell me where you are?"

"I thought you'd already disappeared into your latest assignment."

"No. I declined it. Every operative in the agency would kill his granny for an assignment like that. My contact said I was uniquely qualified. But plenty of my associates could handle it as well—maybe better. And I finally realized what was going on. There was no emergency. The agency was simply shorthanded. Rather than move people around, it was more convenient for them to reel me in."

"Thank God you figured it out," Nicole said. "But I have a question. Last year, when you first moved to L.A., didn't you tell me you'd quit MI6?"

"I did. I was no longer a paid employee. But they had the option of calling me in an emergency. Now I'm closing that option, so I won't be called again."

Nicole was quiet, thinking about what he'd said and whether she could trust him after so many broken promises. Despite everything, she couldn't resist the chance to see him again. After explaining where she was and that her sister was with her, she said, "Where are you?"

"Outside our condo. By the way, there's a sign in front that says 'Keep out. This building has been designated unsafe by LADBS.' What in the hell is LADBS?"

"The city's Department of Building and Safety. That's good news. If they'd condemned it, we would have been forced to tear it down. Instead, we get to repair it. By the way, driving here could take you a couple of hours because the freeways are closed. So we'll order something to eat and wait."

"I love you," he said.

Not sure of her feelings, she said, "See you soon," and hung up.

When she saw Reinhardt get out of his car, she realized it was impossible to stay mad at him. Why did he have to be such a gorgeous man, so sexy, so smart, so kind—perfect in every way except for his inability to commit and his need to chase danger? He was like a kid who wanted to play cops and robbers after all his peers had outgrown it.

As he approached their table, Stephanie stood up and pulled him into a hug. "Hello, Reinhardt," she said. "Oh, my God, are we glad to see you!"

Once Stephanie stepped back, Nicole walked into his arms. For a long moment they embraced, and she rested her head on his shoulder. Finally, they slid into the booth. When they were seated, he reached for her hand and kissed it, then held onto it while she filled him in on everything that had happened.

"What a nightmare!" he said. "You've been through so much. Just experiencing that massive earthquake—I can't imagine anything more frightening. Now, with the murder charges you face, and the homicide detective determined to frame you, we have to get started on your defense. There isn't much time before you're back on the LAPD's most-wanted list."

"The first thing," Nicole said, "is to find a way into my firm's security tapes without being detected. We need screenshots of men from Las Vegas. Someone sent them to collect on Jerry's huge gambling debts. They threatened him with violence. I know they didn't kill Jerry. That was Martinez. But I have a strong hunch these men are somehow connected to his murder and perhaps Diana's. I tried using an app called Lockbit to hack into the firm's security tapes. It was supposed to keep me from being detected. But after a few minutes, I got a warning that I'd been seen and had to shut down my computer."

"Yes, but remember I have special tools—"

"Wait a minute!" Nicole's temper rose. "You told me you were done, that you'd cut all ties to MI6."

"Peace," Reinhardt said, his favorite way of defusing an argument. "Believe me, I've formally submitted my final resignation. But I won't be cut off from certain resources until it's processed. For that to happen, I have to file a report explaining why I'm severing all ties with the agency. When I learned you were in trouble, I was in such a hurry to get back that I didn't have a chance to do that. This means I'm free to use the tools I have with me."

"Even if it's not for official business?"

"I'm not going to tell them, are you?" He smiled. "If we want to start strategizing, we have to move somewhere more private. I've already commandeered a safehouse. Let's go." He stood up, glanced at the check, and tucked several bills under the salt and pepper shakers.

When they reached their cars, Reinhardt said, "Turn over your cells, ladies. We've got to get rid of them. I have replacements for you at the house." While the women were getting out their burner phones, he opened the trunk of his car and pulled out a hammer. He put the phones on the cement path and gave them each several whacks to break them apart. He put the pieces in a trash can at the edge of the parking lot.

"Stephanie," he said, "Would you mind following us in your car?"

"Fine by me," she said. "As long as you keep me in sight. Please don't lose me. I have no sense of direction."

"I'll do my best," Reinhardt said. He and Nicole got into his car, Stephanie into hers, and they started off. Neither Nicole nor Reinhardt felt the need to talk. He rested his hand on her thigh while he drove. She was watching out the rear window to be sure Stephanie's car was in sight.

By the time they were driving through Sherman Oaks, Stephanie was several cars behind them. Then the number of cars between them multiplied, and they lost her. Reinhardt pulled to the side of the road and waited a while, but there was no sign of her.

"What a mess," Nicole said. "She hasn't got a phone, so she can't call us to find out where we are, and we can't call her."

"Don't worry," Reinhardt said. "I slipped a burner into her purse. It has my number on it. I didn't want to mention the phone to her before we set off because I was afraid she'd decide to call someone else and disappear altogether. I'm sure she'll find the burner soon and give us a call."

Once he was out of the Valley and into L.A. proper, he headed west on Sunset Boulevard. and turned north on a side street with hairpin turns that took them up into the hills. The street eventually narrowed to a single lane. At the end was a small development of townhouses. Some were undamaged while three at the end had fallen, knocking each other over like dominoes. The air, cleared by the wind, gave a view of the entire basin from Santa Monica Bay and the ocean to the snow-frosted peaks of the San Gabriel Mountains.

Reinhardt parked in front of one of the undamaged townhouses. While Nicole got her computer out of the backseat, he opened the trunk and retrieved a leather attaché case and what looked like an oversized computer case. The attaché case had a chain he fastened to his wrist. When he noticed Nicole watching, he said, "Old habit. Probably not necessary here, but you never know."

The townhouse's interior was tastefully furnished with glass-and-chrome modern furniture and brightened with colorful abstract paintings and mobiles. There was a great room big enough to accommodate huge parties. The dining room had a long table with seating for twelve. Passing through, they left their computers and the attaché case on the table.

Reinhardt ushered Nicole down the hall and opened the door of a large master bedroom. "This is ours," he said. Next, he led her across the hall and opened another door. "This second bedroom is for Stephanie." It was smaller than the first, but good sized for a bedroom.

"You mean this house has only two bedrooms?" she said.

"Yes, but also a library, office, and three bathrooms. The place was originally designed for a single occupant, but it's now used as a safe house."

"By who?" Nicole said.

"The British Consulate, of course."

Nicole found it hard to believe the consulate would need a safe house this big, unless it was for high-level dissidents seeking asylum. But how often did those come along? It seemed too large for a single occupant, a covert operative, who would presumably be staying a short time. She wondered if it belonged to MI6, a workplace for a team of spies who planned to be around for a while.

"Are you hungry?" he said.

"Not at the moment. I had a big breakfast not that long ago."

"What else do you need? Clothing? Toiletries?"

"You're being terribly practical." Nicole said. She stood on her tiptoes, put her arms around his neck and kissed him.

"I know," he said. "And it's almost killing me. But your sister is going to call any minute. I'll have to go out and find her and shepherd her back here."

The words were just out of his mouth when his phone rang. He pulled it out of his pocket and said, "Hello Stephanie," then "I know, I know. I really apologize for losing you. Can you tell me where you are?" After a brief silence, he went on. "You don't know? Drive to the nearest business or petrol station and ask for their address. As soon as you find out, call me back. I'll be waiting."

"See?" he said when they'd hung up. "We'll have to stick to practicalities until later. Back to your clothes. Do you have enough to wear?"

"I've been wearing the same few outfits since Tuesday. Everything needs a wash."

He ushered her into a laundry room, a few steps down from the kitchen. It was at the top of a staircase that looked as if it led down to a basement. Not entirely seriously, she wondered if this house had a dungeon for torturing enemies of the state. Even though she was curious, she knew better than to ask. Not only would Reinhardt be offended, he'd never admit such things happened. It was up to her to trust him to tell her what she needed to know, even if it didn't satisfy her fundamental need to know everything.

"Your sister will probably need clothing, as well." Reinhardt was saying. "I know someone who can arrange a personal shopper. You'll give her your sizes and preferences. She'll find things you might like and send you screenshots for your approval."

At that moment, Stephanie rang back, and he was out the door. This left Nicole to explore the house on her own. She headed back to the laundry room and continued to the bottom of the steps. The basement was clean and empty as if it had never been used. She noticed a door at the back that might have led to storage space. She was curious but decided not to waste time finding out what was in it. She had a whole house to explore before Reinhardt returned.

The basement had a cement floor with a drain in the center. The drain made her imagination go wild. She pictured the space set up to hold a prisoner. A straight-back chair hung with chains and clamps to fasten around his wrists and ankles. A bare cot with a folded blanket at the foot. This led to something she'd tried to avoid thinking about during her relationship with Reinhardt. As part of a secret enforcement arm of his government, had he done terrible things?

This thought was hard to shake, even after she climbed the stairs up to the main floor and began looking around the kitchen. The oversized refrigerator had a good supply of food. In the dining room, she looked at Reinhardt's locked computer case and attaché case. Each had combination locks that appeared impossible to open. She picked them up one at a time, finding them heavy for their size. She longed to peek inside, but there was no way to do that.

She wandered through the house, looking in cupboards, closets, and cabinets. Most were empty. One closet was filled with towels and sheets, but nowhere did she find anything personal. An hour passed, and she began to worry. What was taking Reinhardt so long to return with Stephanie?

At last they arrived. Stephanie marched in without saying hello. When Reinhardt showed her to her room, she went in and slammed the door.

"What happened?" Nicole said.

"She sent me to the wrong address, and we had a hard time connecting. She's annoyed I kept her waiting. I'm sorry for that, but I did the best I could."

"Don't worry. That's just Stephanie. She'll get over it."

The two of them settled at the dining room table. Reinhardt unlocked the cases he'd brought inside. He opened his attaché case and pulled out two new burner phones, handing one to Nicole and setting the other on the table.

Meanwhile, Nicole was taking in the contents of his case. What she noticed first was a lethal-looking gun, a silencer, and a mesh bag of bullets. A clear plastic passport holder contained a number of maroon and dark navy passports. She couldn't help wondering what assumed names appeared in them and, more importantly, when and under what circumstances Reinhardt used them. There were a number of electronic gadgets she didn't recognize. Then her eyes fell on a bag of what looked like palm-sized black hockey pucks.

She picked one up. "What is this?"

"It's a bug. They were in my first batch of gadgets. They've been outmoded now that we have more sophisticated listening devices. Still, they can come in handy if you're in a rush. They have a strong adhesive on the back. If you attach one to a wall, it will record voices within a twelve-foot radius."

"I've never seen these before," Nicole said. "They'd come in handy in my work."

"Sure. Take what you want."

"Thanks," she murmured, dropping three of the devices into her purse.

He unlocked his computer case and took out his computer. It was bigger than hers and had an unusually large screen.

"First, can you get me into the firm's security tapes?" she said.

Reinhardt got busy on his keyboard, typing in commands before switching to the log-in for her office. After he typed in more commands, the office security tapes appeared on his screen.

"Okay, we're in. Why don't you take over, Nicole. You know what you're looking for."

They traded seats so she could sit in front of his computer. Winding the tapes back in time, she found the men she was looking for and, at last, took screenshots to capture their faces.

"I have some more things I'd like to find on your computer," she said. "I need to look up Martinez and Ronald Blithe, the man who tried to kidnap me, on social media. I didn't want to risk doing it on my computer because those sites track location. Your computer must be untraceable. Right?"

"You bet," he said. "But give me a minute with yours, and I'll make sure no one can see you, much less find your location. It's an app called Non Locatus." He went on her computer and pulled up an unfamiliar browser. "It works like Google. But you remain invisible while you do your searches."

After she went back to her laptop, and Reinhardt to his computer, she turned to him. "Would you mind looking for my friend RJ? I think the initials stand for Robert James, last name Barrett. He rescued me and let me hide out at his place a couple of nights. I'm worried about him. He seems to have disappeared."

He began typing. She'd barely gotten started when he said, "I can't find any RJ or Robert James Barrett. Are you sure that's his real name?"

"Pretty sure. He's an accomplished hacker. Could he have completely erased his presence on the web?"

"Possibly."

"Okay, then," she said. "I'll just have to wait until he gets in touch. I hope he's alright."

They were both silent for a bit, working on the background of Martinez's associates. It wasn't long before Reinhardt said, "I found the Las Vegas contingent and their whereabouts at the times of the murders. They've got the perfect alibi. They were in Las Vegas. And another thing—their boss is Sam Georgiou. He's CEO of the corporation that owns two of Las Vegas's biggest casinos."

Nicole looked for Martinez on Facebook and other social media sites with no luck. But when she searched for Ronald Blithe, she found him. He'd posted several family photos. Nicole stared at the images. It was upsetting to see him as a smiling family man, his wife at his side with their three grown children and a toddler grandchild. Of more interest was a group photo that included both Blithe and Martinez. It appeared to have been taken at a bar. Several other men appeared in the shot, but they were turned away from the camera.

She showed it to Reinhardt. "Looks like these guys are buddies. Maybe they're in with Martinez and the loan sharks who were after Jerry. But, without shots of their faces, it's impossible to ID them, much less figure out how they're connected to Martinez other than the obvious—through their work."

"Good point," he said. "I'm going to hack into Martinez's cell. We'll be able to see his messages and track his location so we can follow him and see who he meets with."

"Would that be safe?"

"Don't worry, my darling. I'm well trained in this." He pulled up an app on his cell and typed for a bit. "There. Now give me your cell."

He installed the app and connected it to Martinez. "He's at home right now," he said. "Once he's on the move, we'll set out after him. Meanwhile, I think Stephanie has settled in. I can hear her TV." He took Nicole's hand and led her down the hall to their room.

At the end of the afternoon, Reinhardt was alerted that Martinez had received a message. It said "530pRH," which the two of them decided must be code for a meeting at 5:30 pm. RH was probably the destination, but they didn't have a clue where it was or what it might be.

"Let's get in the car and head downtown. The meeting could be anywhere, but it's not going to be in these hills or on the West Side."

As Reinhardt and Nicole got ready to leave, he took time to lock up his attaché and computer cases and put them in a closet.

Minutes later, as they drove away, Nicole felt wired, as if they were heading into something of world-shaking importance. She had no idea whether it would turn out to be a major breakthrough or the ultimate setback. But she had the feeling that it would completely change the course of their efforts to prove her innocence.

CHAPTER THIRTEEN

NICOLE MONITORED REINHARDT'S CELL PHONE while he drove. Its screen showed an icon of Martinez's car moving into downtown on a live map of L.A. They were headed there, too. The little car on the map stopped on First Street not far from police headquarters. Reinhardt and Nicole arrived at the spot a few minutes later. The street was empty except for Martinez's car, which turned out to be a white Tesla. It was parked near the entrance of a bar.

The place looked like a dive. On the roof, a sign blinked out the bar's name, the Rabbit Hole. Most of the sign was taken up with a neon white rabbit that disappeared into a black spot at the bottom and popped up again. The establishment's façade was plain except for a small, ragged canopy over the entrance. Reinhardt parked a few doors down. They took out their phones, ready to snap pictures of whoever arrived next.

"Try to get photos of the license plates," he said. "Together with a face shot, they could be useful."

The first car to appear was a vintage red Thunderbird convertible in mint condition. Despite the cool weather, the top was down. The man who got out was what a romance novel might call *tall, dark, and handsome.* He swaggered rather than walked into the bar. Nicole was able to catch a side view of his face along with a photo of his license plate.

After that, five others arrived in short order, two in muscle SUVs, one in a low-slung silver sports car, and two in sedans that looked like—and probably were—unmarked police cars. "Catch the faces closest to you," Reinhardt said. "I'll do the same."

When they compared photos, they had good views of five of the six faces. "Stay here," Reinhardt said. "I'm going to catch the license plates we can't see from here."

She watched him get out, look around to be sure no one was watching, and slowly walk past the recently parked cars. He was heading back to the car when the man who'd arrived in the Thunderbird stepped out of the shadows. It wasn't clear how long he'd been standing there. He went up to Reinhardt and gave him a shove that made him take several steps backward. "Why are you snooping around my car?"

Exaggerating his accent, Reinhardt said, "Pardon me. I do apologize." He sounded calm and congenial, as if he hadn't taken offense at being shoved. "I stumbled. Old knee injury. Iraq, you know."

The man glowered at Reinhardt as he got back in the car. As soon as the door closed, he sped away. Reinhardt looped around the roads surrounding downtown to make sure they weren't followed before heading back to the townhouse. When they walked in, they could hear Stephanie's TV, pumped up to full volume.

Nicole turned to Reinhardt. "Should I ask her to turn it down?"

He shook his head. "Leave her be. She's tired of being here, and she's making it known."

"Right. I'll just look in on her. Here's my phone with the photos and my notes. I'll be right back."

Stephanie was in front of her TV again, following the moves of the yoga instructor on the screen.

"You okay?" Nicole said.

"Just dandy," Stephanie said, echoing what their mother used to say when she meant the opposite. "I adore being locked up by myself with nothing to do."

"Look, I'll be done in a couple of hours," Nicole said. "Then we can do something together—maybe make dinner? He has an amazing assortment of food in the fridge. Why don't you check it out? Make yourself a snack. Chips and dips in the cupboard next to the stove."

"Wunderbar," Stephanie continued in her ironic tone. "I can hardly wait." She got up from the floor and seemed to make an effort to be more agreeable. "Well, did you find anything?"

"Yes, a lot," Nicole said. "I think we'll be able to identify Martinez's buddies with facial recognition software. It will be fun seeing how it works. Do you want to sit in?"

"Why would I want to do that?" Stephanie said. "You don't get it, do you? Being locked up here is crushing my soul. I need to get out of here. How about this? I'll go home and stay by myself. At least I'll have something to do."

"Your house collapsed, remember? So you can't go back there," Nicole said.

"I could stay with a friend."

"I'm really sorry, Steph. I know you're miserable, but the people looking for me are sure to know we're related. If they get their hands on you, they're likely to take you prisoner and threaten your life unless I surrender to them. It's just too dangerous."

"Fine," Stephanie said. "Go away and leave me alone."

"Have at it." Nicole left, resisting the urge to slam the door. When she got back to the dining room, she gave Reinhardt a shrug. "She's reverted to her fourteen-year-old self. But she'll get over it."

Reinhardt had already set up their computers, and they settled down to work. He used the photos they'd taken to trace the men's identities through a sophisticated website reserved for government agencies, top-level investigators, and spies. Each time he found a name, he verified their connection to the LAPD and messaged it to Nicole.

Drawing on her P.I. experience, she began checking out the detectives to see if they could afford their lifestyles on their LAPD salaries. First, she searched the annual salaries for long-time homicide detectives. The top was about $94,000, not a lot for supporting a family in a city as expensive as L.A. Next, she went to county records to see what property was registered to them. Sure enough, their homes were valued at 1.5 to 2 million dollars—quite a stretch on what these men earned. She knew it was possible for some to have inherited wealth or be married to high-earning wives. But all of them? Not likely.

On a hunch, she looked up property records in counties surrounding Los Angeles. Vacation "cabins" were a traditional way for cops, firemen, and other public servants to hide extra income that wasn't on the up and up. Sure enough, each owned property in San Bernadino County near Lake Arrowhead, a popular vacation spot for Angelinos. Their "cabins" were valued between $2.5 million and $4 million. An online search turned up photos of them, large, handsome houses with sizeable yards. The priciest had three floors and two extended decks. It was surrounded by what looked like a forest of fir trees.

When she confirmed the pattern, she showed Reinhardt.

"Now we're getting somewhere," he said. "I'd say these men were being paid very well to do something they didn't want the LAPD to know about. The first person we saw arrive at the meeting today, James Henning, isn't on the police force, and I can't find him online. I recognize him, though. He's the one who came out of the bar and confronted me."

"Is it possible that's not his real name?" she said.

Before he could answer, Stephanie came out of her room. "I'm starving." She sounded even more aggrieved than before. "Doesn't anybody ever eat around here?"

Nicole glanced at her watch. It was 7:30 pm. None of them had eaten since breakfast.

"Good point," Reinhardt said. "Let's take the rest of the night off and celebrate what we've accomplished so far."

"We still don't have a direct connection between the cops and Las Vegas," Nicole said.

"Don't worry. It'll come." Reinhardt took a bottle out of the refrigerated wine rack in the kitchen, while Nicole and Stephanie consulted on which frozen pizza to put in the oven. Once they were sitting around the table, trading stories, Stephanie pulled out of her bad mood, and the evening unfolded pleasantly.

§

In the morning, Nicole and Reinhardt set out at 6:30 a.m., leaving Stephanie asleep and on her own for a few hours. The evening before, she'd promised to stay put. They were hoping she'd keep her word.

Their plan was to stake out Martinez's house and wait for him to leave so they could follow him. When they arrived on his street, Reinhardt parked down the block. They waited a bit before Martinez appeared, bolting out the front door as if he were late for something important.

Reinhardt followed him on roads that zigzagged south toward LAX. Nicole was puzzled. "He can't be going to the airport, can he? I thought it was closed indefinitely because of the quake."

"I think that's exactly where he's headed. By the way, the airport's been open for several days. How do you think I got here?"

"I don't know. Diplomatic flight? Air Force One?"

"Very funny," he said. "I flew coach on Southwest after a connecting flight on Brit Air from Heathrow to Phoenix. They had to get LAX up and running right away. It was a major priority. But flights are limited to smaller planes because the runways are not fully operational, and several of the terminals are too damaged to use. The upside is that there aren't many incoming passengers now. No one wants to come to your beautiful city. Flights going out are booked solid."

"Quitters," Nicole said. "They don't know what they're missing."

"Exactly," he said. "Now let's figure this out. If Martinez is going to Las Vegas, which I strongly suspect, which airline is he likely to use?"

"That's easy. It would be the one you flew in on, Southwest. They have most of the shorter flights in this part of the country."

"Okay, then. I'll pull up to the Southwest Terminal and follow him in to confirm where he's headed. Meanwhile, you take over driving and circle the airport's inner road—"

"Wait!" she said. "No way I can drive your car. It's a stick, and I never learned how to shift. I'll go into the terminal and follow him."

"I can't let you do that. Think about it. What if he recognizes you? We're going to forget all about this and go back to the safe house."

"That's not necessary. I'll only be in there a few minutes. I saw a squall jacket and knit hat in your trunk. Get them out for me before I leave the car. They'll cover me and bulk me up so no one will recognize me. Martinez isn't even looking for me here. Besides, it's a public building with lots of people around. Once I know where he's going, I'll come right out and wait for you to circle back and pick me up."

Reinhardt shook his head. "I don't like this, Nicole. I don't like it at all. Promise you won't linger in there. You'll leave the instant you learn his destination."

"I promise." But her mind was already racing ahead, hatching a plan that could prevent her from keeping her word.

Driving onto the airport's horseshoe road was like entering a medieval vision of hell. Miraculously, the tallest structure, the air controller's tower, was still standing. But signs of the quake's enormous force were everywhere. The top level of the road was gone. Whatever remained had been torn away, leaving a ragged ledge. The biggest terminal at the horseshoe's apex—Tom Bradley International—had collapsed. Its top floor had dropped onto the lower level and left the walls at crazy angles. The sprawling United Terminal across the way had been leveled. Although the quake had hit early in the morning, these terminals would have been busy at that hour. Nicole wondered how many had died there.

Reinhardt stopped the car at the curb of the Southwest Terminal and handed Nicole his credit card so she could buy a cheap ticket that would allow her up to the gates. Then he got his squall jacket and hat out of the trunk and handed them to her. The jacket was heavy enough for a snowstorm and, once Nicole put it on, ridiculously oversized. The black knit hat was too big, and she had to fold up a sizable cuff so it wouldn't slide down and cover her eyes. On her way into the terminal, she caught a glimpse of her reflection in the window. She looked like a very large child wearing hand-me-downs from a much bigger sibling.

Only then did she remember her gun was still in her purse. Weapons were not allowed inside the airport. She'd never get through security. She stepped outside again and craned her neck, looking for Reinhardt's car. It was already at the end of the airport horseshoe, too far for her to call him back. She stepped inside again and dropped her gun in a trash bin. She didn't like having to carry a concealed weapon, didn't like any kind of firearm. But threats on her life had made the gun necessary. It had served her well. She'd almost come to regard it as a good-luck charm.

At the Southwest ticket counter, Nicole pulled out her global entry card, an authorized substitute for a passport, to use as her ID. She kept it in her wallet behind her driver's license. Reinhardt had arranged for it to identify her as Natalie Ilyina, and it had facilitated her escape from Russia at a time when she was wanted by the Russian secret police.

After buying a ticket for San Diego, the cheapest she could find, she went outside to wait for Martinez, who had to park and take a tram to the terminal. Before too long, he breezed in. She followed him as closely as she dared. He was in an enormous rush and walked so fast she had trouble keeping up. She lost him briefly, then caught up at security. After presenting her fake ID to the TSA agent, she followed the detective to his gate. His buddies from the Rabbit Hole were waiting for him. The sign at the gate said they were going to Las Vegas.

That was the moment when Nicole understood what she needed to do. That Martinez and the others were headed for Las Vegas wasn't news nor would it advance their investigation one bit. They already knew the murders were somehow connected to the city's gambling industry. They needed more. Why were these men going there, and why now? Who were they going to see? And the basic question—what were they up to?

The only way to find out was to follow them. She knew the enormous risk she'd be taking and was terrified at the possibility that Martinez and the others might recognize her. But she was certain that the greater risk would be passing up this opportunity by going back to the townhouse and doing nothing. Steeling herself, she went to a nearby customer service desk and turned in her ticket for San Diego. "I bought this by mistake," she told the ticketing agent. "I need a ticket for Las Vegas." She handed over Reinhardt's credit card. The woman ran it and issued the ticket.

Heading back to the gate, she saw that the passengers were starting to board. The detectives were in the first group, reserved for passengers who paid extra to get on first and have their choice of seats. She joined the second line. When she boarded, she was relieved to see her targets sitting in the front. She found a seat at the very back, where she hoped to remain unnoticed and unseen. She'd already turned off the ringer on her phone, but Reinhardt's texts kept coming. "Where are you?" and "You're scaring me," and, "Do not follow him onto his flight."

She messaged him: "I have to do this. Please try to understand," and, "I'm okay. Quit fussing!" When his texts kept arriving, she turned off the phone. She spent the rest of the flight fiddling with the pen from his attaché case, setting it up so she could easily start recording if the opportunity presented itself.

When they landed, the men got off first and disappeared into the terminal. Since Nicole was seated at the back, she had to wait for all the other passengers to get off before she could. Her body was vibrating with impatience. When she was off the plane, she ran all the way through the terminal to the area for passenger pickup, arriving just in time to see them pile into a stretch limousine. She boarded a waiting cab and told the driver to follow it.

It wasn't long before they arrived at their destination—a complex of buildings with crenulated roofs. They appeared to be made of ancient gray stone, but it was probably a veneer of concrete and other building materials. A high window in the tallest tower looked as if Rapunzel might soon hang out her golden hair. Signs posted on each tower identified it as Lucky Castle Casino and Hotel.

Nicole waited until the men went inside before entering. The lobby was a huge, gold-lit room that looked as if it had been lifted from Disneyland. In the center was an enormous fountain surrounded by statues of unicorns, dragons, and other mythical creatures. They weren't cartoon cute. Instead, they bared sharp teeth and looked as if they were about to attack.

The detectives were talking to a clerk at one of the check-in desks. He made a phone call, and they milled around until a well-dressed, silver-haired man arrived. He greeted them with hugs and air kisses before leading them to the elevators.

The elevator was crowded, making it easy for Nicole to slip in without being noticed. Her short stature, she'd noticed, made her all but invisible to other passengers in elevators, especially if she stood at the back. Occasionally, failing to sense her presence, someone would back right into her. Hoping her cloak of invisibility would keep working, she stood at the rear.

She was much too hot in the heavy jacket and knit hat, but she didn't dare take them off. They went all the way to the top floor, the level that traditionally holds a hotel's most luxurious suites. She waited for them to leave the elevator before she hustled out. From there, she stayed a good distance behind them. At the end of the hall, they disappeared through double doors. A discreet gold sign identified it as the presidential suite.

She decided to wait in case they came out again. The corridor was lined with black marble alcoves that featured busts of creatures from a very dark fairy tale. Like the ones in the lobby, these were fierce, not cute. Figuring Reinhardt's jacket would blend into the black marble, Nicole stationed herself in an alcove behind the statue of an emaciated fairy wearing a crown of black, sparkly leaves. It had a rictus grin and was holding a wicked-looking sword.

She hadn't waited long before several young women stepped out of the elevator and headed for the men's suite. They were wearing scant, ostrich-plumed outfits and looked as if they were about to perform in one of the casino's late-night shows. A few minutes later, a parade of carts emerged loaded with food and liquor.

While the doors to the suite were open, Nicole got a glimpse inside. The entry hall included a sparkling fountain and an elaborate crystal chandelier. Considering the food and entertainment that had just arrived, she decided that the detectives weren't going to leave their suite any time soon. She left, went down to the main floor, and found a quiet bar where she could shed the warm jacket and hat. She sat for a while, before deciding to face the music and call Reinhardt.

As she expected, he was furious. Without a hello, he said, "What the hell, Nicole! Are you crazy? After everything we agreed on, you followed him to that casino in Las Vegas. This is the stupidest—"

"How do you know where I am?"

"I followed your phone. Damn it, Nicole! This is the most reckless, irresponsible thing you've ever done. Here's what you're going to do next. You're leaving the casino, catching a cab to the airport, and coming back to L.A. Now, this minute, before you get yourself killed."

"I wasn't calling to ask your permission to be here," she said. "I'm being extremely careful, and they have no idea I'm here. Your coat and hat made a good disguise by the way. I'm just calling to let you know I'll be staying overnight, and there will be a significant charge on your credit card. The rooms here cost the moon. I'll pay you back. But I need to know if there's a limit on your card."

"I'm not going to tell you," he said. "Please be reasonable. I don't want anything to happen to you. These people are extremely dangerous, and they're not stupid. They're sure to notice you're following them. Come home. I'm begging you."

"I'll see you tomorrow." She hung up and turned off the phone.

Back in the lobby, she headed for one of the check-in desks. There was a glamorous brunette behind the counter whose nametag identified her as Erika.

"I'd like to check in," Nicole said.

"Certainly," Erika said. "Do you have a reservation?"

Nicole was prepared. "I do. My name is Madeline Jackson."

After the woman did a search, she gave Nicole a puzzled look. "I'm sorry, but we don't have a reservation under that name."

"Oh, my God," Nicole said. "My P.A. assured me she'd reserved one of your luxury suites."

"I'm so sorry, but I can't find your name in our system. And I'm afraid that all our deluxe suites are occupied. Celebrities and high rollers reserve them months in advance. The good news is that I have superior rooms in other parts of the hotel."

Nicole assumed the tone of a woman who was used to getting what she wanted, when she wanted it. "I didn't come to Lucky Castle to be treated like a tourist. I need one of those suites for just a night or two before I move on. Maybe there's an opening between reservations. Please check."

"I very much doubt that." Erika said. She typed into her computer, then stared at the screen for a long moment. "Well, I'll be—Sorry, I was mistaken. We do have a suite that's empty between guests. It's one night only, so I can give you the reduced rate of only $4,600. Do you want me to reserve a superior room for your second night?"

"Not now. I'll take care of it tomorrow."

Nicole held her breath while Erika ran Reinhardt's credit card. The charge cleared, and Erika handed her a key card. "Suite C on the twentieth floor is yours for tonight. Do you need a team member to help with your bags?" When Nicole shook her head, Erika pointed to an alcove. "The elevator is over there."

"Where do I find a shop that sells women's clothes?" Nicole said.

Erika smiled. "You've come to the right place. Our shopping concourse has many fine shops." She pointed in the opposite direction of the elevators. "Go through that archway and take the escalator to the second level."

Following her directions, Nicole rode up on a cleverly designed spiral escalator. At the top she found herself in an enormous retail mall. She wandered around a bit before spotting a shop window that featured burkas. It struck her that a black, floor-length coverup that hid her hair and most of her face would make a great disguise. Inside, she headed for the section with racks of the black robes. Only when she tried one on and looked in the mirror did she remember. A burka-clad woman wouldn't be walking around by herself in a place like this. She'd have to be accompanied by a man.

She took the burka off and went to a different part of the store featuring more contemporary clothes. From a rack of long-sleeved maxi dresses, she picked out a navy abstract print with a matching scarf and veil to cover her hair and face, all but her eyes. Like the others on the rack, it was $400. It fit perfectly except that it was so long it reached the floor and puddled out, putting her in danger of tripping. She found a saleswoman and said, "Do you do alterations?"

"Yes, madam."

Nicole again used her rich-lady voice. "This has to be shortened so it reaches my ankle. I need it this afternoon—right away, in fact. I'm a guest—"

"I'm sorry, madam. That won't be possible. We don't have a seamstress in the shop. We'd have to send it out—" She stopped talking when Nicole pulled out a hundred dollars of the money Evie had given her and held it out.

"Of course I'll make an exception for you, madam," the woman went on. "It will be ready in two hours. What is your room number?"

This time Nicole wasn't worried about a limit on Reinhardt's credit card, and the transaction went through without a hitch. After she completed the purchase, she went back down the escalator and took the elevator to the top floor to find her assigned room. It was around the corner from the detectives, farther away than she'd hoped, and it was much smaller and less posh. It did, however, have a jacuzzi and bidet in the bathroom, as well as a fully stocked bar and enormous TV in the living room. The best part of her location was that the detectives would have to pass by on their way to the elevator. She turned the TV on low, then got up to look out the peephole every time she heard someone pass by.

Her dress was delivered, but the detectives didn't make an appearance. It seemed they were happy enough to stay in for the night.

§

The detectives passed her room just before 8:00 the next morning. After a beat, she came out wearing her long dress with the scarf and veil so only her eyes could be seen. As the men waited for the elevator, she positioned herself around the corner so she could hear them without being seen.

The men seemed to be suffering from too much of a good time.

"Man, am I hungover," one said.

"Me, too, But those girls they sent. Like, wow!"

"Yeah," said a third. "That was quite a reception. He must be happy with us."

At this point Martinez spoke up. "You, Barker. This is your first time here, so let me tell you something. Pleased or pissed, the boss always makes the same grand gesture when we get here, and I don't think he's pleased right now. I mean, ask yourself, why did he call a meeting this early when he knew we'd need time to sleep off his welcome? But it doesn't matter. We'll carry on like good soldiers, find out what he wants and do it. Remember, best manners. He gets really pissed off if . . ."

"Yeah, yeah," another said. "Drop the lecture. I have a headache."

They continued grousing until the elevator arrived. As they went into it, someone said "What floor?

"Lobby," was the reply.

She waited until the door closed behind them before she went into the elevator lobby and pushed the button for the next car. It arrived almost immediately, and she reached the lobby in time to see them passing the big fountain. They didn't seem to be in a hurry to get to their destination. They were talking in low voices, and she couldn't make out what they were saying. They clammed up when they reached a long hallway with mirrored doors. The men went into an office at the end. A sign on the door said "Sam Georgiou" without revealing his title. From Reinhardt's research, she knew that Georgiou was the big cheese here, owner of the largest casinos in Las Vegas.

Noticing that one of the doors in the hallway was slightly open, Nicole stepped into what looked like a storage closet. She left the door ajar so she could keep watch. After a while, the men came out. Martinez and the others were shaking their heads. One of them made a hissing noise through his teeth, another half-whispered "son of a bitch," only to be shut down by the others. They were silent the rest of the way to the elevator and seemed even more distracted than before. Here they paused, apparently unable to decide whether to go up or down. Finally, one of them murmured, "Hair of the dog" and pressed the down button.

Nicole knew she had to take a separate elevator or risk being spotted. But she could see they were dying to talk about some major grievance they were afraid to discuss near Georgiou's office. She had to record what she was fairly certain they'd discuss once they were alone on the elevator. She got out one of the tiny recording devices Reinhardt had given her, removed the cover on the sticky backing, and stepped into the elevator. She pressed it to the wall to secure it. Then she gave a cry of distress and called out, "Hold the door! I forgot something. I have to get out." The men in the front of the car obligingly stepped out and allowed her to leave.

She waited until their door closed before pressing the button for another elevator. It opened right away. She rode down to the lobby, where the detectives were just exiting their car. When they were all out, passing into the lobby, she stepped inside their elevator to prevent the door from closing. Retrieving the bug, she dropped it in her pocket and quickly walked to the nearest women's bathroom.

After making sure the room was empty, she went into a booth and played the recording on low. Even though she expected it would be bad news, she was shocked by what she heard.

One of the men said, "He's pissed at us because—without his permission—you stupidly whacked Stevens and that girl. Talk about unleashing a hornet's nest."

At that point, someone must have pushed a button to make the elevator pause. There was a clunk, and the loud humming stopped.

"What's the matter with you morons!" It was Martinez. "Stevens was onto us. I'd arranged a loan for him, and he kept missing payments, like he thought our rules didn't apply to him. He wanted to borrow even more, but I said *no*. And what did he do? He figured out I was getting money from the casino for the odd job." He paused a moment before saying. "What? You want the chief to know about my arrangement and figure out that you guys are in on it, too? Stevens was a friend of mine until I tried to make him pay back the loan. Then he threatened to squeal to the brass, so I didn't have any choice. And that girl—she saw me. No choice there either."

"Maybe that's all understandable," said another detective. "But what he's really pissed about is your failure to catch Graves. What's the big deal? All you have to do is grab her, do the deed, and leave what's left of her in the desert. How hard can it be?"

Listening, Nicole felt a chill and an urgent need to get out of the hotel and run.

"I ... I," Martinez sputtered. "It isn't easy. She's one tricky bitch. Blithe owed me a big one, so I sent him to get her. And what happened? He turned up dead, garroted. I know she did it, but I have no idea how. Can't you guys just ..." The rest of the recording was silent.

Nicole left the women's bathroom and rushed through the hotel lobby toward the exit. She had to put some distance between her and these people thirsting for her blood. She planned to go to the airport and catch a flight home. She didn't even dare to take time to return to her suite and get her things.

She passed through row upon row of slot machines and had almost reached the exit when two men in matching maroon jackets grabbed her arms, one on either side. "Come with us, miss," one of them said. "We're going to sit down and have a little chat."

CHAPTER FOURTEEN

THE MEN IN MAROON JACKETS looped their arms through Nicole's, turned her around, and propelled her back through the row of slot machines. "Let me go!" she cried out. "You've made a mistake. I'm a guest here!"

Conversation around them halted. People stopped to stare, and a man stepped forward with his phone out. He snapped a picture of the three of them and said, "Release her this minute, or I'm calling the management."

"Look at our uniforms, sir," one of the men said. "We're security at the Lucky Castle. Our cameras caught this woman cheating at poker. We're going to make sure she leaves the premises."

"That's a lie," Nicole shouted, appealing to the people around them. "Do I look like a card shark? I've never played cards or gambled in my life."

The crowd watched a bit longer before losing interest. Some disappeared through the exit while others headed farther into the casino.

The maroon jackets walked Nicole into a sparsely furnished room that looked as if it had been transported from LAPD headquarters. They led her to the table and made her sit down.

When they sat down opposite, she noticed they were wearing name tags that said *Security* and gave their first names, Bobby and Matt.

"I'll get right to the point," Matt said. "We know you weren't cheating at cards, but our security cameras caught you doing something much worse. You followed some of our VIP guests to their suite on the top floor yesterday afternoon and back down again this morning. We want to know why."

"You're mistaken," she said. "My suite is on the top floor, too. That's why I went up there. And, of course, I had to come back down this morning."

"Come on," he said. "Our cameras caught you trailing them into the executive wing. You were definitely following them. You even took photos of them."

"Okay, okay," Nicole said. "I'd rather not tell you, but here it is. One of those men, Chad Barker, is my boyfriend. He flies here a lot and stays at this hotel. I've long suspected he's been cheating on me and knew it had to be someone here. At this point I've learned everything I came to find out. I was heading to the airport when you dragged me in here."

"Is that so?" Matt said. "If you're really leaving, you must be in a big hurry because you left your things in your suite. How about we arrange a sit-down between you and Mr. Barker? It will give you a chance to straighten out your little tiff."

"That's not a good idea," she said. "I don't want him to know I was here. Besides, I'm going to the airport now, no harm done."

"Give me your phone so we can see those photos," Matt said.

Nicole hesitated, before deciding it was useless to resist. Reluctantly, she handed over the phone.

When it was in his hands, Matt said, "Password?" After she told him, the men flipped through the photos. Bobby spoke up for the first time. "I don't know. These pictures don't seem to have anything to do with Mr. Barker."

"But they do!" Nicole said. "Someone brought half-naked women to the suite he's sharing with his buddies. I'd have to be stupid to think they just dropped in to—"

Matt interrupted. "What exactly were you planning to do with these photos? Blackmail him?" He dropped the phone in his pocket and inclined his head toward the door. He and his partner left, and the lock clicked. She tried to tell herself they were going to discuss the matter, come to a reasonable decision, and let her go. What she feared most was that they'd get Barker and bring him back to confront her. If that happened, she'd be finished. He knew who she was and would readily take her away and carry out the hit.

She looked around. The door was locked, and there was no window or back door offering another way out. All she could do was remain where she was and hope for the best.

It seemed like a long time before the door opened and they walked in. Matt was carrying Reinhardt's squall jacket and the clothes she'd left in her room. To her great relief, Barker wasn't with them. When they were seated opposite her, Matt said, "Okay, here's what we decided. Mr. Barker came here for a good time, and we're not gonna ruin it by making him face some jealous bitch. A driver's outside, waiting to take you to the airport. He's gonna stay until he sees you board a flight heading out of town. Is that clear?"

She murmured her assent.

Enjoying his power over her, Matt put his hand behind his ear, as if he hadn't heard. "I asked you if that was clear."

"Yes, sir!" she shouted.

"That's better. Come with us."

He handed the phone back. "We deleted the photos you took here. You're lucky to be getting your phone back." They latched onto her arms as they had before and marched her out the casino's main entrance. A shiny, black stretch limo was waiting in front. As they pushed her into the second row of seats, Matt had a few parting words. "Just know. You're never coming back here. You've been permanently banned from the casino. We'll be on the lookout."

As the limo pulled onto the busy boulevard, Nicole took in the empty seats surrounding her. She was the only passenger. Her focus shifted to the uniformed driver. Was he really taking her to the airport? Or was he also under orders to bury her in the desert?

She breathed easier when the chauffeur turned onto the access road to the airport. Despite all the no-parking signs, he left his vehicle in front of the main terminal. Inside, they bought tickets, hers for L.A. and his, she assumed, for a cheaper destination that would allow him to accompany her into the boarding area. She took a quick detour at a newsstand and was surprised to find a print edition of the *Los Angeles Times*. She bought one. The chauffeur sat on a bench across from her. They didn't speak, and he seemed remarkably incurious about the way she was being forced to leave. She wondered if this kind of thing happened all the time.

She started reading the paper and was shocked to find herself on the third page under a headline reading, "APB on Nicole Graves Reinstated." The district attorney himself had appeared at a news conference to announce that the hunt was on again. He was quoted saying: "The public should be aware that she is armed and dangerous. If you see her, do not approach. Call 911. We are doing everything possible to apprehend her."

She kept on her headscarf and veil as she boarded and sat down. Then she sent a message to Reinhardt that she was on a plane leaving Las Vegas. He called her back just before takeoff. Although he was short with her, he did agree to pick her up at LAX. He was waiting outside baggage claim when she arrived. They started for the temporary parking structure in the center of the airport's horseshoe road.

"Look," he began. "Following those men was a crazy thing to do. It unnecessarily put your life at risk. I need you to promise you'll never do anything like that again and mean it this time."

"I'm sorry I upset you, but I had to do this or miss the first real chance we've had to prove my case. Wait until you hear what I found. We'd never have gotten it if I hadn't followed them."

By the time they got to the car and climbed in, she'd finished explaining what she'd found out and how she'd recorded Martinez's confession.

"It's just that I've been so worried," he said. "Not only that. I've been kicking myself because this was entirely my fault. I should have been the one to follow them. I can't forgive myself for failing to insist and stop you from going into the terminal. After all, I'm the one who's trained in surveillance. Besides, Martinez and the others have never seen or heard of me, so there was no chance they'd spot me.

"Please don't get me wrong," he went on. "What you did was unacceptable. But I do admire your courage and ingenuity. You would have made a good covert operative." He reached across the gearshift to give her a hug. "Sorry if I lost my temper, but you really gave me a scare. Please, never do that again."

"I won't," she murmured into his neck. They held each other for a long moment before he started the car and drove out of the airport.

"The all-points bulletin is out on me again."

"I know," he said. "Good job with the costume, but you'll have to stay inside from now on."

"Agreed. Do you realize we've just about concluded our investigation? Just one more thing. We have to find out more about Sam Georgiou," Nicole said. "He's the one in charge, and those detectives were terrified of him. They were grousing about their assignment—to bury me in the desert ASAP—but they were determined to —"

All at once she noticed that Reinhardt had turned onto Sepulveda heading south instead of north to the safe house. "Whoops," she said, "I think you turned the wrong way." At that point, he sped up and began to weave between lanes. "What are you doing?"

"Look at the blue car in the lane to our right," Reinhardt said. "Do you recognize the driver? I think it's the chap who met with Martinez at the bar. You know, the one who arrived in a convertible. That car followed me into the airport; now it's right next to us."

Nicole studied the man's face. "You're right," she said. "He's one of Martinez's buddies. Come to think of it, I didn't see him in Las Vegas. I wonder if he's been hanging around, looking for us."

"Hold on," Reinhardt said. "I'm going to lose him." He slowed up, allowing several cars to zip around him into the lane behind their pursuer. The man tried to slow down so his car could remain next to theirs, but the drivers behind him objected to being delayed and started honking. The man seemed to lose courage and sped up again.

When there was a slight break in traffic, Reinhardt slammed down on the accelerator and made a U-turn that barely cleared oncoming traffic. At the next intersection, he zipped into a parking structure and out onto a parallel street.

"I think we've lost him," Reinhardt said.

"Thank God!" Nicole said, although she was still too tense to relax her grip on the safety strap above the door. Her heart kept pounding all the way to Sunset Boulevard. Reinhardt seemed to have forgotten his anger, and they fell into an easy conversation about Las Vegas. She was surprised at how familiar he was with the scene. But it made sense.

He was, after all, a risk taker and, she imagined, had probably done his share of gambling.

When they arrived at the townhouse, Stephanie was sitting on the porch. Her expression made it clear how angry she was. Once they were inside, she said, "Being caged up like this is killing me. I'm going out for a drive."

"That's not a good idea," Reinhardt said.

Nicole piped in, "If someone spotted you, they could grab you, and it would put us all in danger."

"I'm just going to drive around in the hills." Stephanie sounded as if she were about to cry. "If I stop for a walk, I'll choose someplace deserted, where I won't run into anyone. But, if the canyon roads are open, I might drive out to Malibu and look at the water. If I do that, I won't stop my car. I promise."

"Please stay here," Reinhardt said. "Taking a drive is too risky."

"I'm sorry, but I'm leaving." Stephanie shrugged into her jacket and hurried toward the end of the road where Reinhardt had parked her car.

After she was gone, Nicole and Reinhardt gave each other nervous glances. They didn't need to say what they were thinking—that Stephanie's lack of self-discipline could bring all hell down on them.

"Maybe we should have locked her in her room," Reinhardt said.

"Believe me, I thought of that," Nicole said. "But I couldn't bring myself to do it. Now I wish I had."

They had no choice but to get back to work. Reinhardt looked up Sam Georgiou on several databases including Interpol, Nicole searched him on her browser and came up with more information. He was an important man in Las Vegas and the biggest contributor to Nevada's political campaigns, including judicial elections. He'd also been indicted two years before for loan sharking. The jury had acquitted him. Later, an investigation by the *Las Vegas Sun* revealed that four of the jurors in the trial had been employees of his casinos. The paper also reported that Georgiou had long been suspected of having mob ties.

Reinhardt's deep dive on Georgiou confirmed his connection with a notorious mob family operating out of New Jersey. He was also identified as the head of a national association of loan sharks. Loan sharking, the practice of loaning money at unreasonably high interest rates, was illegal in the U.S. and pretty much everywhere else.

"This guy really is the Godzilla of villains," Nicole said. "I think we have enough for me to start writing a report. But I'm hungry."

"Why don't I make my specialty, toasted cheese sandwiches?" Reinhardt said. "It's the only thing I know how to cook. Any idea when your sister will be back? Or do you think she's moved on, and we've lost her altogether?"

"I love toasted cheese sandwiches. As for Stephanie, I doubt she's really left. She wouldn't do that without letting me know. But I'm worried about her. Where can she be?" After Reinhardt disappeared into the kitchen, she went back to the report.

Before long, Reinhardt appeared with a bottle of wine, two glasses, and a plate of sandwiches. It was 9:00 o'clock.

After a sandwich and a glass of cabernet, Nicole said, "I'm just too tired to write any more. Is it okay with you if we stop and pick this up in the morning?'

"I'm done, too," he said. "It's been a long day. Let's go to bed."

§

It was dark when they got up the next morning, and Stephanie still hadn't returned. After they dressed and ate a quick breakfast, they got to work. She wrote the main narrative while he searched for more revelations on the MI6 databases.

By noon, she finished the report and handed it to Reinhardt. After reading it, he said, "This is really solid, and, unlike agency reports, you've made it read like a murder mystery."

"Really?" she said. "Maybe that's my next career, as a twenty-first-century Agatha Christie. But seriously, how are we going to release this in a way the LAPD can't ignore."

"Don't you have a friend at the *Los Angeles Times*?" he said. "He helped you out a while back when you uncovered some corrupt city officials?"

"That was Greg Albee. I left a tip on the *Times* website when I was first running from Martinez. I tried contacting Albee first, but his phone was no longer in service, and I haven't seen his byline in a long time. I don't think he's with the paper anymore. But he's probably still in journalism somewhere. I'll try to find him."

An online search revealed that he was working in the Los Angeles bureau of the *New York Times.* "That's even better," she said. "If we can get him interested, it will be a national story—maybe even international. No way the LAPD can ignore that."

She did a people search and found his new number. When she tried to call on Reinhardt's untraceable phone, she was immediately sent to voicemail. "Please call me back," she said. "I can't leave my name, but you'll remember me from the story I gave you about corrupt city officials. I've got a new investigative piece for you." She left Reinhardt's number.

Around 3:00 p.m., Albee returned her call, and she told him what she and Reinhardt had discovered. "Wow!" he said. "You're already in the headlines for running from the police after being charged with murder. Anything you can share with me will make headlines. I can't wait to hear what you've got. Can we meet at my apartment?" When she agreed, he gave her his address.

Before setting out for Albee's place, Reinhardt insisted she change back into the outfit she'd bought in Las Vegas with the scarf that covered most of her face. The address was in Hollywood, one of the historic art deco apartment buildings on Rossmore Avenue.

"I'll wait here," he announced when he pulled up to the curb. "My presence would just complicate things."

"Right," Nicole said. "He's extremely curious. He'd want to know all about you and why you're with me." She leaned over and kissed him before getting out. After ringing Albee's doorbell, she was buzzed into the building. She figured the face scarf would arouse too many questions and took it off in the entry hall. The place had the slightly stuffy, unpleasant smell common to old apartment buildings. She took the elevator to Albee's apartment. He hadn't changed much since she last saw him. He was still a phlegmatic-looking, middle-aged man. On a closer look, she noticed that his hairline had receded a bit, giving more real estate to the freckles that covered his face. He'd also put on some weight, which made his habitual slouch more pronounced.

"Come on in," he said, taking the envelope she offered containing her report. "Have a seat." He gestured toward the dining room where the table was covered with his computer and a mountain of paper, newspapers, and magazines.

She gave him a brief rundown of what they'd uncovered. When she was done, he pulled the report out of the envelope and flipped through it. "Wow!" he said. "Fifty-four pages, single-spaced. I'm sure we'll have questions. How do you want me to reach you? At the same number you called me from?"

"Right," Nicole said.

"Are you going to tell me whose phone that is? It's not yours, and I couldn't trace it. It seems to be based in Europe. Is that right?"

"The phone has nothing to do with the story."

"No," Greg said, "but it has to do with you, Nicole. Your life looks pretty interesting from here."

"Interesting, yes. Good? Not so much. I'm wanted on a trumped-up murder charge, and the real killer happens to be the detective on the case. There's also a hit out on me, which leads me to the favor I want to ask. I know you have to name me as a victim of a conspiracy between several L.A. homicide detectives and a Las Vegas billionaire. But please don't write about my previous appearances in the media."

"My God," Albee said. "This sounds like a fantastic story. About mentioning backstory in my article. Let's face it. In the last few years, you've been in the headlines several times, and those stories went viral. So you're sort of famous. Of course I'm going to include your history just like any other news outlet would. Why are you trying to deny your past, when it makes you look—well—heroic?"

Nicole sighed, remembering being chased by paparazzi after the last story she gave to Albee. "Whatever," she said. "At least try to limit the number of people who know about this story while you're working on it."

"I'll try to limit it to one editor. I think they'll agree to that. But you do realize that we have to fact-check the story. If I were to tackle an article of this scope on my own, it would take weeks. I'm sure you want it to appear as soon as possible. That means I'll have to enlist help from several other investigative reporters."

She knew any requests she might make would be brushed aside, but she couldn't help asking, "Can you give me an idea when this will run?"

"You know the drill," Albee said. "We can't just go on your word. So we have to fact-check. That's the biggest hurdle."

"Last time I gave you a story, it took—what—ten days, two weeks? It's not going to take that long this time, is it? I mean it can't. There's an APB out on me and a murderous police detective after me. I'm in incredible danger."

He seemed to soften a bit. "I'm sorry. I really am, but I have no idea. I'll try to send you daily messages about our progress."

On that unsatisfying note, Nicole left and went downstairs. She felt let down and deflated, as if all the air had gone out of her.

"How did it go?" Reinhardt said once she was in the car.

"It's going to take at least a few days for them to fact-check, write it up, and run it in the paper. So we have to hide out for a bit—hopefully not too much longer."

When they arrived at the safe house, Stephanie's car was in front. She and a man were sitting inside.

At first, Nicole thought the man was holding her sister prisoner and had come to kill her, perhaps all of them. But when the two emerged from the car, she saw that Stephanie's passenger was Peter, the manager of the Blue Lagoon Lodge. While the sisters were staying there, she'd noticed that he and Stephanie had been flirting, but she hadn't picked up on any deeper connection.

Stephanie was all smiles. "Sorry to break your rules, Nicole, but I just had to see him. Reinhardt, this is—"

Reinhardt interrupted. "Get inside!" he said, ushering them into the house. Once they were inside with the doors locked, he turned to Stephanie. "Give me your keys. I'm going to move your car away from the front, in case someone picked up your trail. Everyone, stay here!"

While they waited for him to return, Nicole was having mixed feelings about Peter. She was upset that Stephanie had made the long drive to pick him up, stayed overnight, and brought him here, risking the chance of being followed. On the other hand, she was glad to see her sister take an interest in him. He seemed kind, reliable, and solid, quite a contrast to Stephanie's previous boyfriends. They'd been an ill-groomed and ill-mannered lot, generally unemployed and/or involved in the drug trade. None of these relationships lasted more than a few months, and restraining orders were sometimes part of the breakup process.

Once they were settled on the couches in the great room, Stephanie said, "Can Peter stay here with us? The Blue Lagoon Lodge shut down, and he needs a place to sleep. He has friends in WeHo who'd take him, but I'd rather not have to drive him there."

Nicole exchanged glances with Reinhardt. Both were horrified at the idea of her leaving again.

"Of course," Reinhardt said. "Peter, you're most welcome to stay. We have plenty of room."

Stephanie stood up, gesturing for Peter to follow. "Come," she said, "I want to show you my room." They disappeared down the hall and shut the door after them. The lock clicked.

Reinhardt and Nicole laughed. "That was fast," she said. "Stephanie isn't exactly shy when she's got a new boyfriend."

"He seems a good sort," Reinhardt said. "And look at us! We have a free afternoon." He got up from the couch and led Nicole to their bedroom where they found enough to occupy them until dinnertime.

When Nicole entered the kitchen, Stephanie was already there and in a chirpy good mood. The two of them defrosted a cut-up chicken, mixed it with potatoes and herbs, and baked it. They'd just sat down at the dining room table when the lights flickered off and on several times. Reinhardt got to his feet and made a shushing sound. Then, in a whisper, he said, "Quick. Get down. That was a signal that our property line has been breached. Someone's outside."

CHAPTER FIFTEEN

REINHARDT BENT OVER so he couldn't be seen through the window and hurried to the front door. Looking through the peephole, he said, "It's Martinez's mates. I can't see him, but he may be out there, too."

Next came clicking noises as the intruders started trying to pick the deadbolt locks on the door. After grabbing his attaché case and their computers from the closet, Reinhardt silently beckoned everyone to follow him. When they were passing through the kitchen, he whispered, "Don't worry. They'll never be able to crack those locks."

He hurried them to the basement stairs. As they descended, they heard loud banging, which meant the cops had given up on the locks and were trying to break down the door. "The door is solid steel and impregnable." This time Reinhardt spoke out loud. "They'll probably try the window next. It is breakable, but it's bulletproof, so it will take them a while. Let's hope they remain outside long enough for us to get away."

In the basement, Reinhardt went over to the door Nicole had noticed on her earlier visit. He pulled keys out of his pocket and opened it. It wasn't a storage closet beyond the door. Instead a dark tunnel came into view. A light went on as soon as he stepped inside. After the others followed him in, Reinhardt pressed a button on the wall. The door closed and several heavy-weight deadbolts clicked into place.

Nicole was scared but, at the same time, certain Reinhardt could pull this off. Watching how smoothly their exit from danger had been planned, she smiled. *Of course*, she thought. *What would an MI6 safe house be without a secret tunnel as an escape hatch?*

The tunnel was brightly lit and painted white, so the walls almost seemed to glow. They walked for a while before reaching the end. Here they came to another door, which Reinhardt unlocked using the same key. The door opened into a dark space. Once again, the lights turned on when they stepped inside and found themselves in a garage that housed a shiny gray sedan.

"The car is here in case of emergencies like this," he explained. "Get in, everyone." Once they were seated, Reinhardt pressed the ignition button. Nothing happened. He tried again but the engine remained silent. "What the—" he said, getting out of the car. Peter followed, and the two looked under the hood and started poking around. After perhaps thirty seconds, Reinhardt went to Nicole's side of the car. Since she couldn't lower the window, she opened the door, so she and the others could hear him.

"Of all the rotten luck," he said. "The battery's dead. Wait here. I'm going to check something."

He headed for a side door of the garage. Peter started to follow, but Reinhardt signaled him to stay put and quickly exited. He was back almost immediately. "We're switching to plan B. Those men are now in the house searching for us. They left their SUV parked in front. I'm hoping we can use it to get away, but we have to move fast." Under his direction, they got out of the car and coordinated their positions. At his signal, they rushed to the vehicle. Nicole breathed a sigh of relief when they found its doors weren't locked.

They started to get in when they heard someone cry out: "No you don't."

One of the detectives had raced down the steps and grabbed the back of Reinhardt's jacket, dragging him away from the SUV. The two men began to fight, punching each other wherever they could. At one point the detective knocked Reinhardt to the ground. "Drive away," he shouted at Nicole and the others before he and the cop started punching each other again. The key was in the SUV's ignition, but no one made a move to start it.

The men were on the ground, hidden by a hedge, when the sound of a gunshot was heard. Nicole held her breath until Reinhardt got up, apparently unhurt, and dashed to the car. He'd barely gotten in when more detectives, alerted by the gunfire, emerged from the house.

Reinhardt immediately started the engine and gained speed as the men started shooting at the departing vehicle. Nicole and the others ducked down. Soon they were too far away for the bullets to reach them. Leaving the townhouse and the detectives behind, Nicole felt a cool rush of relief. They were going to be okay.

Once they reached Sunset Boulevard, Reinhardt sped up even more, taking a winding route south to the beachfront community of Venice. Here, he turned off on a street lined with ramshackle houses. Nicole was surprised such houses still existed here. Venice was prime residential property, known for its quaint canals, beautiful beach, and frequent waves of gentrification.

He pulled up in front of a small, clapboard house that was in marginally better shape than its neighbors. "Sorry about the accommodations," he said. "But it's the only other safe house available at the moment. It's meant for an individual operative spending a night or two before moving on. I'm afraid it's going to be a bit cramped for us."

They went in, and Nicole and the others looked around. The house was bare-boned, not only smaller but many pegs down from the townhouse where they'd been staying. There was only one bedroom, although the couch in the living room could be folded down into a bed. The TV set was small and there was no dining room and no kitchen table, just a bar with two tall stools in a corner of the tiny kitchen. Fortunately, Reinhardt and Nicole no longer needed to be glued to their computers, so the lack of a table wasn't an issue.

The galley-shaped kitchen was so small that it looked like it belonged in a mobile home. But the real problem was the complete lack of food in the house. Reinhardt's first act as host was to call the mysterious person who arranged things for him and set up discreet deliveries of groceries and restaurant meals. On the first night, a pizza was delivered, along with several bottles of wine and enough breakfast fixings for a week.

Stephanie and Peter opted for the TV set, which meant they would sleep on the couch. Nicole and Reinhardt took the bedroom. They spent most of the first night in pillow talk. She started out half-joking about her plans for the future. "You know, I won't be returning to the detective agency, even if Melanie manages to keep it going. Instead of looking for another job, I've been thinking about starting my own firm."

"What a great idea!" Reinhardt said. "I have to admit I'm not loving paper-pushing at the consulate."

"Why did you keep insisting you were perfectly happy?" she said. "I always suspected that job wasn't doing it for you."

"I was—I am happy to be here with you. I didn't dislike the work, but it was a bit unchallenging. Your new venture sounds exciting. Will you take me on as a partner?"

"Wouldn't that be fun—working together in our own firm?" she said. "Of course you can be my partner. What an asset you'll be!"

"As long as we're dreaming . . ."

Nicole interrupted. "Who said I was dreaming? Think about it. I know how such firms are set up. I'm a licensed P.I. myself, and I know several others no longer employed by Colbert and Smith, who'll be looking for work. What's to stop us?" They batted about ideas for half the night and woke up a little after 11:00 a.m.

Still exhausted from their narrow escape the previous day, the four of them watched TV most of the day. In the evening, they played cards with a couple of decks found in a hall table. For Nicole, it felt incredibly good to zone out.

The next morning, her feeling of relief had worn off. There were more stories in the paper about the APB and reports of sightings of Nicole, several of them in Venice, where she actually was. The day passed without the promised update from Albee—and a second day, still with no word. Everyone was on edge. Adding to the problem was the impossibility of avoiding each other in such close quarters.

Once again, Nicole used Reinhardt's phone to call Albee. He sounded distracted when he picked up the call. "Albee," he said.

"Hi," she said. "It's Nicole—in case you've forgotten."

"Oh, Nicole. I was just about to send you a progress report."

"You can just tell me. Any progress?"

"Well, sure. Lots. But right now it's with the paper's attorney. We can't move forward until we get the go-ahead from him."

Nicole, who knew too well how lawyers could delay decisions, realized she had to move things along. "I'm sorry. That's not good enough," she said. "No more delays. I'm in extreme danger here!" She departed from the truth, drawing on a previous experience with the tabloids. "XHN told me they'll publish it right away, as a story with my byline, no fact checking involved."

"Wait a minute, Nicole. You know we can't do that. Can't you give us a little more time."

"No."

There was a long silence before he said, "Alright, can you give me a day? I'll see what I can do.

§

The next morning a call came in on Reinhardt's cell. He and Nicole were sitting on their bed struggling to read the paper against the blare of Stephanie and Peter's TV in the next room.

Reinhardt answered, then handed the cell to Nicole. "It's Albee," he murmured. "Let's see if I can get them to turn down the TV so you can hear."

"So your mysterious friend is a Brit," Albee said. "Who is he?"

"It's still none of your business," Nicole said. "What's happening? Are you finished? Has it been approved?"

"Almost."

"Almost?"

"They want me to interview you on video for our online edition," Albee said. "You know, like the last time we worked together."

Nicole winced at the idea of opening up her life again to the public and, worse yet, to the tabloids. "No way!" she said.

"Well, the editors think a video would attract a larger audience. Isn't that what you want?"

"No. All I want is for those detectives, especially Martinez, to be arrested and locked up."

"But . . ."

"No buts," she said. "I'm sorry, but I'm not doing it."

There was a long silence, which she read as Albee's disappointment that she wasn't going to give him the interview that he and his bosses wanted. Finally, he said, "Okay. I'll let you know when they schedule a slot for the story. It's going to take up part of the front page and at least two inside pages. So it depends on how much space we have on a given day."

"No," she said. "I need it to be in the paper tomorrow, or the day after at the latest."

"Nicole, you're asking the impossible."

"I'm sorry, Greg. Take it or leave it."

"Okay, okay. I'll get back to you this afternoon and let you know if we can do it."

It wasn't until 9:00 that night that Albee called. "You got it," he said. "It's going to appear early tomorrow. Oh, and I have a couple of tips for you. I heard from the D.A.'s office that they've ended the APB on you, based on the new evidence you gave us."

"Wait," she said. "I thought you were going to keep that information under wraps until the story ran. How did the police get hold of it?"

"We had to get a comment from the top brass," Albee said. "Don't complain. As a result, you're no longer wanted by the police. You're free to come and go. And there's something else. Get down to police headquarters downtown by nine o'clock tomorrow and wait out front. There's going to be a perp walk that will gladden your heart."

"I'll be there. Thank you so much, Greg," she said. "Thanks for everything."

"*De nada*," he said. "Are you finally going to tell me who this guy is?"

"Sorry, Greg. Cannot do.

"Someday?"

"Maybe."

Once she hung up and spread the news, the feeling of doom disappeared from the tiny house. The four of them decided to have a victory dinner with food and a couple of bottles of champagne delivered from a super-expensive Venice restaurant. As she picked out what she wanted to eat, Nicole took note of the prices on the menu where an a la carte entree could cost as much as $95 and side dishes like rice ranged from $16 to $23.

§

All four set out early the next morning so they could find a parking spot on the busy streets near city hall, the court buildings, and the police headquarters. At 8:00 a.m., when they arrived, there was no indication anything unusual was about to happen. They stationed themselves on the broad path in front of the square, gray monolith that housed the top brass and inner workings of the LAPD.

It was unusually chilly, forty-two degrees with rain in the air. Soon a crowd started gathering. Nicole wondered how people had found out about the perp walk and if they knew the arrestees were not only cops but detectives on the elite robbery-homicide squad.

Nicole felt someone rest a hand on her shoulder and turned to see who it was. A woman she didn't recognize was standing there, dressed in a black quilted coat with a fur-edged hood. To Nicole's surprise, the woman drew her into a hug, exuding a strong scent of lily of the valley. When she let go and pulled back the hood, Nicole recognized her from the day of her arrest. It was Detective Breanna Jones, Martinez's partner.

"I'm so sorry about what happened to you," Jones said, pulling her hood back up. "Martinez wasn't following any of LAPD's protocols when he arrested you. I could see he was railroading you, and I was concerned about what might happen to you. When you became a fugitive, I sent you a message asking you to get in touch with me."

"I saw it," Nicole said. "I'm afraid I misinterpreted it. I thought it was an attempt to get me to surrender to Martinez."

"Yes," Jones said. "I was afraid you'd think that. At the time, I was hoping the two of us could turn him in for dereliction of duty. He'd completely ignored the rule that requires detectives to consider all suspects and not charge someone just because they happened to be at the scene. Of course, I had no idea at the time that he'd gone completely rogue and was guilty of the murders himself. Again, I want you to know how sorry I am that I didn't stand up to him."

"Thanks, Breanna," Nicole said. "I could tell you didn't agree with him, and I really appreciate your concern. We've had some scary moments, but at least I had the satisfaction of shutting him down myself, and things worked out."

"But they might not have. You could have been killed. I blame myself for not reporting him. But I'm still a rookie. Not only would they not listen to me, but it would have ended my career as a police officer. I heard about their arrests on the grapevine, and it was a real shock. I'm so relieved you were spared, and their crimes caught up with Martinez and the others. At least there is some justice in the world."

Nicole introduced Jones to Reinhardt and the others. They chatted for another forty-five minutes until they heard sirens, faint at first, then growing louder, announcing that the perp walk would soon take place. Six black-and-whites pulled up to the curb, and uniformed officers got out of each one and pulled a detainee from the rear seat. Some were already dressed, but a couple were wearing trousers and shoes but no shirt or socks, much less a jacket to keep out the cold.

Jones squeezed Nicole's shoulder when Martinez finally appeared. At first, the sight of him sent a shiver through her, which quickly changed to a sense of triumph. Despite all his efforts, she'd survived, and he looked thoroughly defeated. He was wearing pajamas in an unlikely print of Santa Claus, reindeer, and sleighs. She guessed it had been a gift from his family, although she found it hard to imagine him in the role of husband and father.

He seemed deeply humiliated, shrinking back and dropping his head in an attempt to keep photographers from getting a face shot. Nicole wondered what was going on in his head. Did he have regrets at the terrible things he'd done, or was he only upset about being caught?

As they went by, several detectives glanced at her and, seeming to recognize her, looked away. When Martinez caught sight of her, he straightened up, pulled back his shoulders and gave her a look that made her think of the evil eye—intense eye contact accompanied by a particularly ugly sneer. He maintained it for as long as he could, twisting his head around after he passed. On her part, Nicole met his eyes and stared back, forcing herself not to blink until he entered the building.

When all the cops and their prisoners disappeared inside, Nicole and the others started back to the car. As soon as they got home, they gathered around Reinhardt's large-screen computer to read Albee's story about Nicole's ordeal and the crime wave unleashed by the gang of detectives.

Later that day, the top story on the TV news showed not only the perp walk, but the events leading up to it. Most notable was a clip of Martinez's reaction when two uniformed cops arrived at his house. He ran out the back door, doing exactly what Nicole had done when Martinez came to arrest her. This forced the cops to chase him for several blocks before catching and subduing him. Nicole laughed until tears ran down her face.

The other arrestees were more cooperative when the cops came for them. The final scene showed them being delivered to police headquarters. Reinhardt, Peter, and Jones could be seen standing in front of the building. Nicole and Stephanie made quite a spectacle, grinning, jumping up and down, and waving at the camera. Nicole was surprised. She had no recollection of waving, nor could she remember seeing any cameras there. She'd been too elated by the sight of Martinez, subdued and defeated.

The story reported that the detectives were facing charges of murder, attempted murder, and conspiracy to commit murder. A trial was expected in six to nine months. Bail was denied, which meant that they'd have to spend the time behind bars. According to the court, they posed a threat to the public and potential trial witnesses.

There was still no mention of the death of Ronald Blithe, the homicide detective who'd tried to kidnap and kill her. That meant she'd succeeded in erasing any trace of herself in his car. At this point, she doubted the police would ever figure it out. For that she was grateful, although she still felt bad about his death.

As the program continued, Nicole was happy to see that coverage of the quake's destruction only occupied a small segment of the news. The focus had shifted to stories about the city's recovery—restored services, government assistance in rebuilding homes and businesses, the reopening of roads and several freeways. It seemed that the city was getting back on its feet just as Nicole was reclaiming her life.

Three Months Later

It was the first Sunday in May. The sun was out, a bright blue sky was framed on the street by purple jacarandas, red-blooming eucalyptus, and the ubiquitous tall, skinny palm trees. Nicole and Reinhardt, both in their PJs, were drinking coffee in the breakfast room of the house they'd moved into the week before.

The townhouse had been sold. Even with structural damage, the property had been worth a good deal to the development company buying up homes in desirable neighborhoods around the city.

Nicole was thinking about their wedding. It was set for mid-June, just six weeks away. She glanced at the to-do list on her iPad, and then at Reinhardt, who was absorbed in the morning paper.

"What kind of flowers should we have?" she said. "Stephanotis, of course, but what else? Orchids or roses?"

"Hmmm?" he said, without taking his eyes from his paper. After she repeated the question, he looked up. "I don't have an opinion on that. It's your choice, darling. Whatever you fancy."

She was mildly annoyed, not just by his lack of interest but his condescending tone. Clearly weddings weren't his thing. It was up to her to make these decisions. She had a flicker of doubt. Wasn't the pomp and ceremony of the wedding a bit silly? A waste of time and energy, not to mention money?

"Okay," she said. "On another topic. We have a couple of things to do this week so we can move forward on our new detective agency."

He folded his paper and straightened up. "I'm all ears."

"Okay. Next we have to get the office furnished and equipped. I'll get in touch with the furniture leasing company and take care of that. Why don't you get the computer equipment and hire someone to install it and set up our network?"

"Good idea. Too bad your friend RJ never surfaced. He'd have been perfect for the job."

"I still wonder what happened to him," she said.

"It's my theory that the police were after him for something he'd done—something unrelated to the charges against you. Perhaps he's disappeared into a new identity with an assumed name. We may never find him. From what you've said, I have the impression he's a survivor, who will probably land on his feet. As for the rest of us, we've pretty much walked away unscathed."

"With a few caveats," she reminded him. "There's the loss of RJ, of course, and Joanne still isn't speaking to me. I warned her that helping me could result in the charge of accessory to murder, and that's what happened. The charge was eventually dropped, but only after she spent five days in the women's jail. That's enough to rile up anyone, and I do feel bad about it. I sure hope she gets over it." Instead of dwelling on the loss of her friends, she got up and settled on Reinhardt's lap, her head against his shoulder, her arms around his neck.

"Just think of the great things that are happening now," he said. "Our lovely new home, the start of our own detective agency. We're so lucky—lucky you survived that terrible earthquake, the murder charges, and Martinez. You're amazing—do you know that?"

She shook her head. "I put it down to luck. Looking back, I can't believe the risks I took. I could just as easily have ended up dead. And we're lucky to have found each other and be about to marry." She resisted the urge to say *finally.*

"Amen." He tightened his arms around her.

More challenges would not doubt be ahead, but at that moment she was entirely at peace.

ACKNOWLEDGMENTS

I WANT TO ESPECIALLY THANK Bill for reading each draft of this ever-changing book. Special thanks go to my other technical advisors: Jeff Boyarsky, my brother-in-law, a retired defense attorney, who helped me with the workings of the judicial system; Cathy Watkins, my P.I. friend, who did double duty as an editor and consultant on private investigators. Extra special thanks to my first readers, who caught plot glitches, and embarrassing errors and made suggestions that helped this become a better book. They are my sister, Susan Scott; Kitty Felde; Esther Eastman; and Claudia Luther. And thanks to all my friends for their continuing interest and support.

Thanks also to Leslie Schwartz for her account of her experience in the Lynnwood Jail for Women in Los Angeles in her excellent book, *The Lost Chapters: Finding Recovery and Renewal One Book at a Time.*

ABOUT THE AUTHOR

THE BIG SHAKEUP: A Nicole Graves Mystery is Nancy Boyarsky's seventh mystery. Before turning to mysteries, Nancy coauthored *Backroom Politics*, a *New York Times* notable book, with her husband, former columnist and city editor of the *Los Angeles Times*. She has written several high school textbooks on the justice system as well as general-interest articles for the *Los Angeles*  *Times' West Magazine, Forbes*, the *California Journal*, and *McCall's*. She also contributed to political anthologies, including *In The Running*, about women's political campaigns.

In addition to her writing career, Nancy was communications director for political affairs for ARCO. Aside from writing mysteries, Nancy is producer, director, and sound engineer for the podcast *Inside Golden State Politics*.

Readers are invited to connect with Nancy at:
nancyboyarsky.com.

THE NICOLE GRAVES SERIES
BY NANCY BOYARSKY

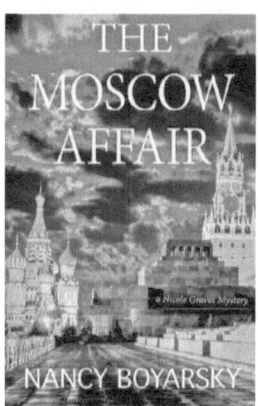

Enjoy the nail-biting adventure, suspense, romance, and humor of
the Nicole Graves mysteries

www.ingramcontent.com/pod-product-compliance
Lightning Source LLC
Chambersburg PA
CBHW031027260626
47153CB00017B/2741